SIGHTSEEING

MICHAEL ONOFREY

CL◢SH

Sightseeing, stealthily and meticulously explores Paris and art in a tale that delves into questions of personal choice and identity with a knowing immediacy that has us questioning our own perceptions and views of art and storytelling.

ED MEEK, AUTHOR OF *LUCK, WHAT WE LOVE* AND *SPY POND*

A mystery woman lures a willing stranger into a fantasy world where time is fluid, and art informs life. With its noir intrigue reminiscent of French new age cinema and its masterful prose, this remarkable novella will keep you guessing.

ALEXIS RHOME FANCHER, AUTHOR OF *ENTER HERE* AND *JUNKIE WIFE*

Onofrey's prose has a mannered veneer that is made strange, made fascinating by how exacting and mysterious it is. Fans of Kazuo Ishiguro, or *Dead Ringers*-era David Cronenberg, here's a book for you.

ALEX HIGLEY, AUTHOR OF *OLD OPEN*

Sightseeing is a beautiful and mysterious exploration of our connections to art and story. Lovers of Paris, Impressionism, and dream-like narratives will find themselves enticed by a daring novel that reads like a painting. *Sightseeing* captivates like the masterpieces it evokes.

CONTENTS

ONE

He sits on a park bench, art of the Orsay swimming in his head—colors, perspectives, eroticism, mystery—as if they possessed him. It is a warm, hazy day in Paris, and he notices her. A woman standing a few feet to his left. How long she's been there he doesn't know. She is looking at him with intent. Is there a connection? This thought seems to pass from him to her, for she says, "Why did you leave me?"

"Leave you?" he questions.

Short black hair, shiny and thick, hugs her head, complexion white, arms thin. She's slightly younger than he is, mid-thirties for her, late thirties for him. She speaks the same English as he does, North American. Articulation of "Why did you leave me?" telling him this.

She shifts her weight from foot to foot and this causes him to look down at her footwear because he hears squeaking, and now he sees why. Her feet are in a pair of new huaraches, leather yet to be broken in. The park is quiet. The creaking leather renews his awareness of this, a small park caught in the laze of midafternoon.

"Have we met?" he asks.

She tilts her head and looks at him.

"I mean, I can't remember meeting you."

She glances around the park, her eyes lively. Two people are on a bench across the way. A third person is stretched out on another bench and appears to be napping.

"Was it in Amsterdam?" he ventures. "I was there a few days ago. Or was it in America?"

Her eyes return to him and she says, "Well, if you don't know."

He's losing her and he doesn't want to do that, he wants her.

"I was in the Orsay until about fifteen, twenty minutes ago," he says, "and all those paintings, Impressionists and Post-Impressionists and Modernists, are dancing in my head. It's like I'm still seeing those colors, those images. They're my favorite painters. Even in Amsterdam it was the Van Gogh Museum I was mostly interested in."

She cocks her head to the side. Her neck is long. It strikes him that she is posing, her head atilt, her face without expression. Her eyes have settled.

"Would you like to sit down?" he says and gestures.

The bench is made of strips of metal that are painted green. She walks in front of him and sits down and lets her shoulder bag drop onto the bench. When she passed in front of him an acrid scent wafted, perhaps dried sweat. But now it's gone. Her clothing is clean, a buff-colored skirt to just below her knees and a green blouse with white buttons down the center.

He looks at her and he sees that she is looking out at the park. Buildings, rising close by, loom. Recently green short grass is already worn to dirt in many places, or maybe the grass never has a chance to sprout in those places. Utility is the park's attraction—a dozen leafy trees, benches of the same number. He imagines baby strollers, old people, dogs, and kids kicking a soccer ball. A four-foot-high chain-link fence, painted green, defines enclosure, gates missing from points of entrance and exit, remnants of hinges at the sides of those openings. What can she be looking at?

"A name," he suggests. "Perhaps your name would help my memory."

She brings a hand up and unbuttons a button to enlarge the opening at her collarbone.

"I'm Wayne," he says and smiles, but she probably doesn't see his smile because her view remains unchanged—the park and its inertia.

"I'm planning a daytrip to Giverny. I want to see Monet's house and garden. I'm thinking of going in the next few days," he offers, as if this might spur conversation, or maybe even a self-invite on her part. But she doesn't react to Wayne's words in any way, acknowledgement absent. Wayne feels he's talking to himself. He turns his head and looks at the park.

"I have an open itinerary," he tells her, or tells the park.

"Why are you here, Wayne?"

He looks at her, but her eyes continue to embrace the park.

"You mean in Paris?"

"Okay, in Paris."

Bafflement constricts Wayne's face. Finally he says,

"Any number of circumstances could have brought me here."

She turns and looks at him.

"Perhaps we could . . . clarify," Wayne says. "Like—I'm here alone. Is that your situation, too?"

She seems to have listened to this, and now she seems to be contemplating a response.

"Do you mean in this park, or in Paris, or in general?"

Wayne smiles. "In Paris."

Her face remains neutral as she says, "Yes."

"Yes? So you're alone?"

"In Paris."

Wayne moistens his lips with his tongue.

"What about in general?" Wayne asks.

"Yes," she replies.

"So you are single, by one means or another."

"You are extremely intelligent, Wayne."

Her speech is slow, each word pronounced, so even though it's North American English it's not TV English. Wayne feels akin to this because he speaks the same way—slower than TV. More energy enters Wayne's smile. But then there was her enunciation of "extremely intelligent" which brings to mind sarcasm and thwarts Wayne's smile.

"What about in this park?" Wayne asks. "Are you alone in this park?"

"I'm sitting on the bench with you," she says.

He is looking at her, but it's more than that, for he discovers that he's staring at her.

"So are we, you know . . .?"

Her view returns to the park.

"Going to continue? Maybe do things together?" Wayne asks.

"I was standing next to you in the museum."

He looks at her anew, at her profile, lines of which resemble a painting.

"You mean in the Orsay?"

"Yes."

"I'm sorry. I didn't notice."

"You were looking at a booklet and looking at the paintings and I was next to you, one painting after another."

"You were?"

She sits, looking at the park.

"Well . . . I was really into those paintings."

"That's where we met."

"In the Orsay?"

"Of course."

"But . . . we didn't talk or anything."

"I was next to you. We were looking at the paintings together."

Her view swings away from the park to find Wayne's face, a somewhat tanned face, a clean-shaven face. Sandy hair is combed straight back.

"We took a break and went to the museum café. The tables were very close together and that big clock was on the wall above us. You had espresso coffee and a croissant and so did I."

Wayne listens to this. But now that she is looking at him with a sense of intensity there is also her face to contend with. Thick black eyebrows and the bowl-like cut of her black hair set her white complexion off in a luminous way. A pair of hazel eyes vibrate like tropical insects. Thin creases, branching out from the corners of her eyes, disturb her portrait. Her mouth moves with distinction.

"Then we were back at the paintings again in those beautiful rooms."

Wayne swallows and he feels his throat move.

"I was at your side."

Wayne waits for more.

"Finally we left the museum," she says. "We didn't cross the Seine. We stayed on the left side. Quickly we were on narrow streets, like we were lost. We went into a small café and stood at a zinc bar and had café au lait. You went to the restroom and so did I, but there was only one restroom. So I had to wait until you came out before I could go in. I went into that narrow restroom and when I came out you were gone."

Her mouth stops moving. Her lips, though, are quivering.

"Why did you leave me, Wayne?"

He is stupefied.

"Finally, I found you in this park."

"I'm sorry," he says.

Tears drizzle down her cheeks, but she doesn't sob or jerk or convulse. Her eyes are flooded and whenever she blinks there's a surge of tears. Wayne reaches across and puts his arms around her and she falls against his chest. She begins to weep, her body against his.

"Why did you leave me?"

She is crying and Wayne is holding her.

Wayne says, "I promise I will never leave you again."

TWO

She stops crying and straightens. Wayne withdraws his arms from around her. She looks right to left around the park. From her shoulder bag she extracts a pink handkerchief that she uses on her damp cheeks. The whites of her eyes are reddish. She sniffles and brings the handkerchief to her nose, but doesn't blow her nose. She sits for a moment and then returns the handkerchief to her shoulder bag. It is a leather shoulder bag with a flap that hitches with a clasp. She stands up and puts the strap of her shoulder bag over her shoulder. She looks down at Wayne, and in this way Wayne stands up.

They start walking toward an opening in the fence. Exiting the park, she again looks right to left. She puts her arm through Wayne's arm as they walk. She is composed. Wayne thinks he probably looks that way too—composed. She doesn't seem to be leading him and neither is Wayne leading her. They are walking on a narrow sidewalk that's on a narrow street that's lined with apartment buildings.

A man, walking a small dog, approaches from the opposite direction. This forces them to go sideways against a wall to let the man pass. The man nods thanks as he goes by. They remain standing with their backs against the wall, graffiti-marked. Their view is of the street, parked cars on one side. It's a one-way street.

"I'm hungry," she says.

"Me too," Wayne replies.

She leans forward to look past Wayne. Perhaps she is looking at the man with the dog who has continued down the sidewalk. Maybe the park is his destination. She straightens and looks at Wayne's face. An eye-to-eye moment ensues. Eclipsing this, she raises herself up on her toes, huaraches squeaking. Wayne bends his head down. They kiss. Her tongue slides into his mouth. He follows her. They embrace and their eyes are open.

There are the sounds of somebody walking by on the sidewalk, shoes, probably leather, on concrete. But Wayne can't see the person. All he can see is the closeness of a face—cheeks and eyes. Her eyes are very wide. Wayne imagines his are that way too.

They finally break the kiss but they continue to embrace.

"We are in Paris," she tells him.

Wayne almost laughs, but the seriousness of her eyes cancels this.

"Yes," he says, which seems to satisfy her because she smiles, teeth short and in a neat row. Her lips glisten because of saliva. No lipstick. She seems plain, but she isn't.

Their arms come away from each other and they begin walking again. This time she holds his hand.

They are on the shadowed side of the street. At the end of the block traffic moves on a wide street. When they reach that busy street they stop. She looks one way and then the other, and then she looks across the street.

The narrow street they have walked on does not continue on. It dead-ends at the busy street. Shops across the street occupy the first floor of a moderately tall building. They turn to the left and walk without saying a word. The sidewalk is wider now and occasionally there's a café with tables and chairs outside.

They enter the third café they come to, but why they passed the previous two cafés is not verbalized, and in the same way there isn't a pause or exchange of words as they bypass outdoor seating to go inside and take a table next to a window, which looks out onto the outdoor seating area and the sidewalk. Perhaps this choice, indoor seating, is in consideration of her very white skin, sunburn a concern.

After they are seated she looks around the café attentively. Maybe she is trying to beckon a waiter or a waitress. Posters on the walls proclaim art exhibitions. A chalkboard lists items and prices. A clock shows three-fifteen.

A waitress comes to their table, beige hair to her shoulders. On the underside of her left forearm a fat Buddha resides as a colorful tattoo.

Wayne reaches for the small French phrasebook he keeps in the breast pocket of his shirt, but his companion's voice stops him; she is speaking French to the waitress, who takes in what is being said without replying, although she does nod to indicate understanding before departing. This new development concerning language has Wayne thinking that maybe his companion is from Quebec, but of course there are any number of people in the United States, or Canada in general, who speak French. Perhaps the woman sitting across from him, who is again looking around the café, spent a good portion of her childhood in France or Belgium or Switzerland. Maybe her parents were expatriates living and working in Europe.

"Where did you learn French?"

The café isn't busy. Two men are standing at the bar. A few tables are occupied.

She looks at Wayne with deliberateness, and she says, "We have already established rules by way of precedent about the past, which is everything before the Orsay."

"What do you mean?"

The waitress comes to their table and sets down two bottles of mineral water along with two stemmed glasses. The waitress then returns to behind the bar.

"We are not to speak of that time before our meeting in the Orsay. Or, to put it another way, if we wish to speak of the past, it begins at the Orsay."

"I can't recall having made that agreement."

She picks up one of the bottles of water and pours water into the two glasses.

"That agreement was made in the park, if not before."

She sips from her glass of water. Wayne sips from his glass of water too. Wayne then looks at the bottles on the table.

"This water tastes really good," Wayne says.

"Of course. Why wouldn't it?"

Wayne takes another sip to check to see that it still tastes especially good. Perhaps it was simply a first-sip experience. But no, the water still tastes noticeably

good. He doesn't recognize the brand of water. A rico-
cheting thought has him wondering if his companion
lives in Paris.

"Have you been in Paris long?" Wayne asks.

A sigh of exasperation registers on her face.

Wayne says, "Oh. Is that a before-the-Orsay
subject?"

"Of course."

"So . . . what I know is that you've been in Paris
since . . . when we looked at paintings together in the
Orsay, at least since then."

She smiles.

"But when we were in the park I told you about
my being in Amsterdam, which was before the
Orsay." Wayne smiles with satisfaction, teeth slightly
gapped.

"How did I respond to that?"

Wayne tries to recall what her response was, but he
can't remember.

"Well," Wayne says, "there it was. It was something
before the Orsay—Amsterdam."

"Please don't mention it again, okay?"

He looks at her. She is serious.

"It's been acknowledged that you're an intelligent
person, Wayne. We don't need to go over this any
further, do we?"

The waitress shows up with two plates, an omelet
on each plate. Cradled in the crock of her arm is a
basket with a cloth napkin that half-enfolds a few
pieces of baguette that are angularly cut. After she sets
the plates and basket down she takes two sets of silverware, respectively wrapped in a paper napkin, from a
pocket of her apron and sets those down next to the
plates. The waitress says something, and Wayne's

companion says something in return, *merci* part of it. The waitress leaves.

"I ordered for us," she says.

"Yeah, I kind of figured that." Wayne motions with his hands and says, "But you know, this is great. I would have probably ordered this myself."

"I know."

Wayne looks at her. Her face has a mild smile. Wayne says, "Well, this looks great."

"Yes," she says and unwraps the napkin from around the silverware.

They begin eating, upon which Wayne comments, "Super!"

They go at their food with gusto, but then Wayne's fork pauses. He says, "What if I didn't like eggs?"

Her chewing is hardly interrupted as she answers, "Then I would have been mistaken."

Wayne's fork remains stalled as he listens to this— its simplicity, its straightforwardness, its casualness. He resumes eating and it's not long before the omelets and bread are finished, remnants of bread used to wipe residue oils from their plates.

"If you gave me a name, it'd be convenient," Wayne says.

The two men at the bar leave the café. She looks at them, and then she watches the men through the window as they turn right and walk along the side-walk to disappear from view, which is Wayne's view as well because his eyes have gone back and forth between her and the two men. Wayne wants to see what his companion sees, wants to know what she pays attention to. With the men gone, Wayne watches her eyes shift to find Wayne's eyes.

"How about Diane?" she says.

"Diane?"

"Yes. Is that okay?"

"Well, yeah, I suppose. It's your name, right?"

A violent sound erupts outside. They both look out the window. A blue car has clipped a parked car and the blue car is spinning to a halt, but then a small white car in back of the blue car hits the blue car broadside on the passenger side. Both cars jump with the impact.

As the cars settle there's a soft silence as if the scene were pausing, and that's what Wayne feels, an interlude, but he knows this will fill rapidly with reaction and comprehension. He turns and looks at Diane because he wants to see this on her face, quietude and its evaporation. He is not disappointed, for what he sees is so well sketched—blankness, concern, fear. Diane is in pain. Anguish contorts her face.

People in the café come to the open doorway that spills out into the outdoor seating area where people are rising from their seats. On the sidewalk pedestrians have stopped to look at the accident as well.

The driver of the white car emerges, a fat man who looks confused, but then he looks angry as he approaches the driver's side of the blue car, a new Peugeot.

The accident has Wayne's attention, yet at the same time he senses that Diane is fidgeting. His view swings to Diane. She's getting a wallet out of her shoulder bag. Her face remains grimaced as her fingers frantically dip into the wallet to wrest out a bill. She gets to her feet while jamming the wallet back into her shoulder bag and flipping the bag's flap closed, clasp left undone. She starts away from the table briskly, leaving Wayne to stand up in a hurry and then to scramble in an attempt to keep up, for panic possesses Diane and it's infused with the intent of flight.

Diane comes up to the waitress and thrusts the bill out for the waitress to take. The waitress, who is standing in the doorway of the café, looks down at the bill and takes it as if on automatic, but then her eyes pause, which constitutes a moment of comprehension in terms of math.

"*Merci,*" the waitress says, but Diane is already past the waitress and is shoving through people who are standing in the outdoor seating area and then more people who are standing on the sidewalk, Wayne trailing. Diane goes left, which is the direction of the traffic, a one-way street, but the flow of cars has stopped because of the collision. Diane continues at a clip, Wayne catching her up and trying to get a glimpse of her face.

"What's wrong?" Wayne asks while Diane continues on, her expression far from composed, yet different from moments before in the café. She looks angry and watchful, and it's the watchful that connotes fear. She turns to look back without breaking stride, so it's an awkward looking back over her shoulder. Wayne, too, looks back, which gives rise to the expectation of someone behind them, but all he sees is the crowd on the sidewalk in front of the café and some people in the street at the blue car. It is a typical accident and Wayne imagines someone calling the police and maybe an ambulance.

Wayne's view returns to straight ahead while checking on Diane's face continually, which is where he now sees objective. Odd, because he should have noticed this before along with the rest of it, for it was there all the time—to get away from the accident as quickly as possible. It's that spectacle that is hounding them, and it is that which they are fleeing from.

If he could only ask about the past—a traumatic car accident or maybe a terrorist shooting at a café. It's right there, almost out of his mouth: Did you witness something before, in Paris maybe? And what follows this is a question for himself: Why am I sticking to these rules—nothing from the past, nothing before the Orsay? Is it that I don't want to upset her by breaking the rules? Or maybe I don't want to upset her by drudging up a harrowing recollection? Or is it something else, something I can't finger, something about perception or learning or understanding or point of view? Something about myself or about her or about the two of us together?

THREE

They continue down the sidewalk. But then . . . are they nearing a tourist destination perhaps? Musée Rodin maybe? For there about a half dozen boys, ten, eleven, twelve years old, hanging out in front of a shuttered storefront as if waiting for . . . They are looking at Wayne and Diane. They are scruffy, and isn't that part of their reputation along with harassing tourists for money or picking pockets or running off with cameras or purses or bags? It's been reported that they even enter museums to execute their cunning. These boys . . . on a sidewalk in Paris. It's like they are living up to a reputation. It's like they are mimicking a status.

Wayne looks at Diane to see what her reaction is and finds she is back to no-expression. In addition, her pace has slowed to what might be considered normal walking. She does seem to be looking at the boys. She buckles the clasp on her shoulder bag. Wayne's eyes return to the boys who have given up their nonchalance in favor of direction, for they are coming out onto the sidewalk proper.

Diane is doing something. Wayne looks. She has shifted the strap of her shoulder bag, so that it now runs diagonally across her chest instead of hanging from a shoulder. The boys wait in a certain manner, each having assumed a post that will collapse around Wayne and Diane as they walk along the sidewalk to enter the boys' domain. It is practiced; it is learned. But where did this tutelage come from?

Wayne and Diane could turn and walk in the opposite direction, which would be the direction of the café and the auto accident. But what would that mean? And what would it bring? Aside from revisiting the scene of the accident, it might bring the boys like wolves, for surely they have a contingency plan for such occasions —a couple of tourists hurrying away on a street where no foreseeable help is available.

They continue on, and Wayne feels he might have to step forward to deal with an unpleasant, frenzied situation, and this could be the boys' strategy, for while Wayne is involved with two or three of them the others would be snatching at whatever they could get from Diane, yanking and pulling and trying to get into her shoulder bag. The boys, having taken up entrapment positions on the sidewalk, are menacing in their expressions.

Someone is approaching from well behind the boys, a middle-aged woman in a dark dress who has a white plastic bag hanging from one hand. But the woman is rather far away. And besides, what could she do to prevent this, or to help once a melee begins?

Diane and Wayne enter the boys' web as if conscripted and the boys collapse the circle. Diane stops walking and Wayne stops walking. And here it is: Diane barking out a burst of guttural language that stops the boys and changes their expressions and then has them departing in a quick step to turn into a walkway between two buildings. They are gone.

Wayne is dumbfounded. "What did you say?"

"I told 'em to fuck off."

Wayne blinks his eyes while looking at Diane. Where did this argot come from? How did that venomous voice evolve? What is the source of such knowledge?

They resume walking. The woman in the dark dress with the white plastic bag drifts by as a nonentity. She no longer possesses relevance. The neighborhood, too, has lost whatever it had before—a tourist enclave, Musée Rodin, or whatever.

Wayne asks a question for the sport of conversing, "Is this street Rue de l'Universite?"

"I don't know. You're the one with the guidebook."

How does she know he has a guidebook tucked into one of the many pockets of his cargo pants? It's a Paris guidebook, which is different than the booklet he was looking at in the Orsay, which is about the art in that museum. The Orsay booklet is also in a pocket of his pants. But the Paris guidebook? Maybe she saw him looking at it in the park before he noticed her. Yet he can't remember looking at that guidebook in the park. Perhaps she simply assumes he has a guidebook.

"If this is Rue de l'Universite," Wayne says, "and we keep following it, we'll wind up in the vicinity of my hotel."

"Your hotel?" Diane says. "That's something we need to talk about."

Wayne kind of smiles.

"I imagine you can switch your room from a single to a double."

"I imagine the same thing. Actually, that's what the desk man asked me about when I checked in, single or double, even though I had reserved a single. The bed is a double bed."

"They will be happy to receive additional money," Diane says.

"The man at the front desk, which is really just a counter, speaks a little English."

"Is there a window in your room?"

"Yes, a small window. It looks out on a street. A café is across the street."

"A toilet and a shower in the room?"

"Yes to both."

"We will proceed to your hotel after we do some shopping."

"Shopping?" questions Wayne.

"Of course."

Wayne shrugs a shoulder.

"I need essentials," Diane relates.

"Essentials?"

"Yes. I have nothing."

"Well, what about at your hotel? Don't we need to go to your hotel to pick up your things?"

"No."

Wayne looks at her.

"I can buy all the necessary items between here and your hotel."

Wayne hesitates and then replies, "I see."

FOUR

They resume walking, and after a block and a half they enter a small shop where they find a selection of vintage suitcases. A petite woman with a wrinkled complexion tends the shop. Her cheeks are rosy with rouge. Her lips are red with lipstick. The suitcases are not cheap. Diane selects a medium-small one that has thin stripes that alternate between tan and black, a cloth texture. Opening the suitcase, a lining of satin-like material glimmers, a shimmering burgundy. Diane pays for the suitcase. When they exit the shop a little bell jingles, door-movement tripping the bell.

"Would you mind carrying the suitcase for me, Wayne?"

"Not at all."

They continue on. The suitcase is light. Its handle has the comfortable feel of stitched leather.

Diane stops in front of a shop window. Two dresses are on display. Diane and Wayne breeze into the shop. A young woman comes forward to greet them. Hardwood flooring accentuates open floor space. Dresses on hangers are along one wall. All the garments look to be made of cotton—flower prints, colorful abstracts, individual brushstrokes. Diane holds a couple of dresses up in front of herself while looking at a full-length mirror, salesclerk alongside with deliberate expressions of approval, and of course French is the language, which is so fitting given the occasion. It's like poetry. Diane buys two dresses that are put into separate slim boxes and then into a stylish paper bag that has rope-like handles. The shop's name is scripted on the side of the bag.

So now Wayne has an empty suitcase in one hand and an upscale paper bag hanging from the other hand as they continue along the sidewalk. Diane takes an interest in a shop that features lingerie. Mischief plays on her face while entering the shop. Wayne stands off to the side near the door. Diane looks at bras, or . . . brassieres, for the word sounds French.

A stiff, gray-haired lady and a more current woman with a relaxed posture constitute staff. It is the casual woman who approaches Diane while the other woman stands and appraises Wayne. Three pieces are selected, red, black, and white respectively. Diane and the lithe woman move on to panties. The older lady, while looking at Wayne, begins a lecherous grin. Wayne can't take it anymore. He goes outside to stand on the sidewalk where he gazes at traffic. When Diane leaves the shop a bag not so different from the bag from the previous shop is at her side, rope-like handles in her one hand.

A hat shop is next, a red beret purchased. A shoe store yields a pair of black pumps and a pair of sport shoes. In a souvenir shop a white T-shirt with the Eiffel Tower silkscreened on its front is chosen. At a knickknacks store Diane selects a pair of studious glasses, frames perfectly round and made of faded yellow plastic, lenses without prescription, clear glass. A cosmetics store: lipstick and nail polish. And then there is a fragrance retailer, front door carved hardwood with panes of cut glass contributing to the shop's luxury. Opening that distinguished door produces an aromatic breath.

"My hotel is just down the street here," Wayne says, which seems to coincide with the end of shopping.

"I forgot to ask," says Diane. "Is your hotel clean?"

"Yes. Small and clean and neat. In the morning there's complimentary coffee, a little cup of coffee and a croissant at the front desk, the front counter."

They have turned left onto a narrow street. A shop with a perfectly symmetrical cross outlined in green neon signals pharmacy.

"This is just the place I was looking for," Diane says, while stopping in front of the pharmacy. "I will purchase a toothbrush and toothpaste and soap and hand lotion. You will purchase a box of condoms."

Wayne sets the suitcase down on the sidewalk and reaches into his shirt pocket.

Diane says, "What are you doing?"

"I think the word for condoms is in my phrasebook."

"*Préservatifs*," Diane says. "Repeat after me: *Préservatifs*."

Wayne repeats.

"Walk around and look," Diane instructs. "It'll probably be written in English as well as French on the box. Or ask the clerk."

They enter the shop, Wayne with the suitcase and a couple of bags, Diane with a couple of bags as well. They separate, each going in a different direction as if to disguise their alliance. It's a small shop and from behind a counter a woman in a white lab coat watches their meanderings. The woman's temperament is quick in proclaiming impatience, for she yaps something out, to which Diane responds. The woman comes from behind the counter to point at something on a shelf. Diane steps over to the shelf. Wayne has glanced at the woman, but has now returned to scanning little boxes in search of *préservatifs*.

The woman's image remains in Wayne's mind, a frightful, formal image—starched lab coat, narrow glasses, taunt complexion, copper hair pulled back into a bun at the rear of her head, and even though she is attending to Diane, Wayne feels her scrutiny as he leans forward to examine box after box where the word "*laxatif*" keeps appearing, which gives rise to the word "laxative" in Wayne's cognition. Wayne hears the woman and Diane conversing. He turns and looks. The woman is back to behind the counter with Diane in front of the counter. Diane has her wallet in hand and is pinching a bill out.

And then there she goes, out the door of the shop, to do what? Stand on the sidewalk and peer through the window to see how things go with Wayne? Perhaps Diane's into cruelty, or humiliation. Or maybe it's humor she seeks. There is an ongoing question: Who is Diane?

Wayne snatches a glimpse of the lab-coat woman and finds she is staring at him. This prompts a second look. What is it? A smirk, a grin, a leer? Perhaps she is in need of entertainment. Here she comes, black shoes tapping out a march on the shop's hard linoleum. She arrives in no time and suddenly there is language at Wayne's face, a mixture of poetry and harassment. Wayne is lost in the beauty of sounds tripping out of the woman's strict mouth. Her eyes are small and severe, and Wayne can't determine their color. Does she know Wayne is a foreigner? Perhaps she has mistaken him for French. After all, he entered the shop with a woman who speaks French, but that woman is now gone, which might explain why she left—to divorce herself from a clumsy foreigner, thus claiming no relationship. Where is Diane?

The woman stops speaking. She is almost smiling, but this doesn't soften her face. Her chin is sharp and abrupt. She raises a white hand in the direction of the shelves in back of Wayne. She utters a word that sounds like *laxatif.* Is she asking a question? Yes, she is asking a question. But Wayne doesn't have an answer. But then he does. He attempts: *"préservatifs."*

She tilts her head, a questioning attitude. Wayne repeats the word, but it feels like a thorn in his mouth. The woman looks at him in a more penetrating way, like maybe he is asking for narcotics, and for all he knows he might be, for it was Diane who gave him *préservatifs.* Wayne needs to consult his phrasebook. He sets the suitcase and bags down. The woman watches this with interest. He gropes for the phrasebook inside his shirt pocket and then fumbles with its pages in search of "condoms."

He feels himself sweating. He needs to calm down in order to focus and locate the word. The woman starts speaking, which draws Wayne's eyes away from the book. The woman stops speaking, and there it is again—a bobbing, rhythmic question. In desperation

Wayne begins pantomime with his hands, which go down to the area in front of his crotch where his fingers imitate the unfurling of a condom on what might be something sticking out in front of him.

The woman watches this. Someone enters the shop, but the woman's eyes behind her severe glasses don't leave Wayne. Wayne's hand, though, has stopped. He, too, doesn't look at whoever has come into the shop, for the lab-coat woman has arrested his attention with a roll of her pharmaceutical eyes. She takes a couple of steps and makes a turn. Wayne leaves his packages on the floor and follows her. She nods toward some shelves and walks away. Small boxes, varying in size and color, are before Wayne's eyes. *Préservatifs* is clearly legible, and so is the word "condoms."

FIVE

They stand on the sidewalk two doors down from the pharmacy.

"Did you make out okay?"

"No problem."

"That's good," Diane says and turns toward the window of the shop they are in front of.

"What do you think of this vest?" Diane asks. "Isn't it nice?"

A half-mannequin resembling a midget, naked and beige, is in the display window, the window's only feature. No arms, no head. Only a bust with a unisex appearance. Fitted on the mannequin is a black vest made of heavy material, goats' wool perhaps. All the edges are stitched with thick red thread, Bokhara red.

Wayne nods.

"I must have it," Diane says and looks at Wayne with a challenging, argumentative expression as if Wayne were going to object to the purchasing.

And so Wayne almost feels like saying, "Well, isn't it a little expensive, darling?" Like maybe they're an established couple, husband and wife perhaps, which would dictate a position of influence on Wayne's part. Wayne finds himself double-checking his and Diane's association.

"Well, if you must have it, you must have it," Wayne says.

Diane smiles and emits a little giggle and stands up on her toes and kisses Wayne on the cheek.

The vest has been purchased and they are back on the sidewalk, another tidy bag added to their collection. Wayne looks at the half-mannequin in the window. A shirt or vest will soon be covering its nakedness, for the shop's goods are shirts and vests and hats from either North Africa or from places east of Istanbul. Wayne reflects on how he began to step forward to pay for Diane's "must-have" vest because he somehow felt that it was his gift from him to her, probably because of Diane's little giggle and tiptoed kiss. But Diane stopped him by saying, "Don't be silly," and got out her wallet and paid for the vest.

"Are we near your hotel?" Diane asks.

Wayne looks down the street in the direction they are headed.

"We turn left up there," Wayne says, "and then there's some small streets. You see the Eifel Tower? It's this side of the Eifel Tower on a small street."

"Then let us be on our way," Diane says as if buoyed.

"On our way" entails a stop at a foodstuffs shop where they buy "provisions"—cheese, wine, bread, and so forth. The sun has sunk well into the western sky. A rosy hue has begun over the city. When they stop walking, Wayne points across the street. "It's through that doorway. Reception is on the second floor."

Wayne points again, this time upward.

"You see that window on the third floor, or in Europe the second floor. That's the window of my room."

Diane looks upward with sharp interest.

"So you have a view of this street?"

"Yes."

"How lovely."

As Wayne steps into the street, Diane says, "Wait. Let's go into the café here and have a drink and arrange things."

"Arrange things?"

"Yes. I need to pack the suitcase."

Diane goes through the open doorway of the café. Wayne follows. Diane chooses a table and sits down on a padded bench against a wall. Wayne sits opposite her on a chair, and since there are two chairs he puts the bags he's carrying on the extra chair. Diane does the same with her bags, puts them next to her on the padded bench. A waiter arrives and Wayne hears Diane pronounce the word "Kronenbourg," which tells Wayne Diane's ordering beer.

The suitcase is upright on the floor next to Wayne's chair, but now Diane asks for the suitcase and Wayne passes it around the table to her. Diane shoves the bags away from herself to make room for the suitcase on the bench. The bench runs the length of the wall, small tables arranged along its length. The café isn't busy. Only one other table is occupied, while at the bar two women stand. Diane opens the suitcase.

The waiter, a young man with pimples on his face,

comes to their table and sets two glasses of beer down. He departs without delivering any sort of expression except boredom. Diane breaks off her activity with the suitcase to pick up her glass of beer and sip. Wayne does the same, sips beer. Diane returns to taking clothes and sundries out of bags and putting them in the suitcase. Wayne watches. Diane motions for the bags on the chair next to Wayne.

Diane is very pragmatic, empty paper bags getting folded neatly to lie flat on the bench. Wayne sips his beer in contentment. When Diane is through she closes the suitcase and snaps its brass clasps shut. She then picks up her glass of beer and looks at Wayne and smiles.

"Now we're ready to proceed to your hotel."

Wayne smiles.

Two men and three women come into the café. The men go to the bar, the women to a table. Wayne can't see the bar unless he turns sideways, which he is tempted to do because that's the direction Diane is looking. Diane's face has changed from a look of pleasure and expectation to a look of concern.

"Aren't those the two men that were in the café where we had the omelets, the men that caused the accident?"

Hearing this, Wayne turns and looks even though he knows he won't be able to ascertain if they are the omelet-café men or not, for he has no real idea what those men looked like. Nevertheless he looks, and all he sees are two men, one very large, the other medium. The medium man is in blue overalls. The big man sports loose gray pants and a yellow short-sleeved shirt. Both men are in their forties and they are in conversation with each other. The barman is setting glasses of beer down in front of the men.

Wayne turns back around to look at Diane. Diane

glances at Wayne with a pair of quick eyes, which return to the men at the bar.

"But what do you mean, 'caused the accident?'" Wayne asks.

Diane doesn't look at Wayne as she answers, "That terrible automobile accident."

"Yes, I know, but . . . How could those men cause the accident?"

Diane answers impatiently, "They caused the accident by causing it. How else does anyone cause anything?" Diane then adds, "It's the big one in the yellow shirt. That big head on his neck."

Wayne doesn't turn to look, for he knows. The man has a large oblong head, black stubble on top of it, a crew cut. His neck is thick and his cheeks hang like bunting.

"Let's get out of here before there's another accident," Diane says.

Wayne wants to understand what's going on, but that endeavor evades him. Diane is fumbling inside her shoulder bag. She brings out her wallet. She opens the wallet and pulls out a thicket of bills. Money in hand, she thrusts her hand across the table to in front of Wayne.

"Here," she says. "Take this so we don't have to think about who pays for what. You pay for things. Pay for the beers and let's get out of here."

"What do you mean? I have money."

"Take this," Diane demands while shaking her hand, "because I'm out of here."

Diane drops the money on the table and scoots along the bench while moving the suitcase before her. Wayne picks the money up. Diane stands, suitcase in hand. Wayne locates a price-board and scans it for

Kronenbourg. Jerking his head back around, Wayne sees Diane striding through the doors of the café. Wayne gets to his feet. The waiter is on his way. Looking down at what's in his hand, Wayne sees the green of one-hundred-euro bills. He shoves the bills into one pocket and reaches into another pocket to get out his own money, which is in smaller bills.

Out on the sidewalk Wayne discovers Diane has crossed the street and is standing next to the doorway of the hotel. Wayne hears the waiter's voice in back of him. He turns to find the waiter standing with the folded bags in his hand. Wayne takes the bags from the waiter without thinking. The waiter issues a shrug and goes back into the café.

Wayne crosses the street and comes up to Diane, who is peering through the plate-glass door of the hotel, stairway beginning about five feet back.

"I think we are all set to go upstairs now, Wayne."

"If I have to register your name, should I use my last name?"

"Sure. Why not?"

"Wayne Wilks and Diane Wilks."

"Sounds good."

"What if they ask to see a passport?"

"We'll go to a different hotel."

SEVEN

Diane's first reaction to the room is to go to the window and look out. It isn't a large window, only about two feet by two feet. Curtains, an opaque beige, are pulled to the sides. Outside the day is dimming. After a moment of looking, Diane flips a small latch and slides one side of the window open.

It is a double-paned window and there's a screen in the opened half. Wayne, having set the bags down, watches Diane as she leans forward to scrutinize the neighborhood from the opened side of the window, which not only allows for air but sounds.

"Paris is like this," Diane comments.

"Like what?" asks Wayne.

"You need only turn a corner and walk a block or two and the commotion of the city disappears. A web of small streets, quiet locale despite nearby attractions —Seine River, Eiffel Tower, Musée Rodin, Les Invalides. There's a neighborhood feel as opposed to a thoroughfare feel, an enclave escaping the clamor of tourists and the spectacle of history. It is this that keeps the city alive. People live and work and make love and die here. Even now."

Wayne listens to this monologue with mild surprise while looking at Diane's back as she looks out the window.

"It is current and art is generated. But it's not the history of the art in the museums that inspires such imagination. It is the looking, the real-time, direct looking at those pictures and sculptures, and at the city's bridges and buildings, and at the sunsets and rain-glistening streets. Cafés with people, food with taste, lovers with frantic flesh.

"Paris is not a relic."

She turns from the window and looks the room over—bed made, side tables neat, a few lamps, a writing desk, a couple of chairs, a small refrigerator. She goes to a door and opens it and inspects the bathroom.

"I will pee," she states.

While Diane is in the bathroom Wayne counts the money she gave him—twenty-one hundred euros.

When Diane emerges from the bathroom, she says, "I want to unpack. Why don't you take a shower, Wayne? I will shower after you."

And so, as if conscripted, Wayne takes a shower while thinking about Diane's capacity for arranging things, romance lacking, yet with the suggestion of more to come. Is there an agenda she's working with, a plan, a script in which drama will unfold?

Wayne comes out of the bathroom with a light cotton robe around himself, a Japanese *yukata*, blue dragons on a white background, and he sees that Diane has transformed the writing desk. Wayne's hair is damp. Diane is placing two chairs next to the desk.

"How lovely," Diane comments while indicating Wayne's robe.

It is the flowers on the desk that renovate it, red poppies in a water glass, but the food contributes to the makeover as well, as do two stemmed glasses and two white plates, all of which were part of "provisions."

Diane picks up a few articles of clothing and goes into the bathroom.

Wayne opens a bottle of water and goes to the window and looks out. Lights have come on. He looks down at the street, café across the way. Raising his view, he can see between a couple of buildings to his left which gives him a wedged panorama. The Seine is in that direction. It must be the Right Bank that's twinkling in the distance. Turning back around, he looks at the room and raises his bottle of water and sips. Anticipation, which has been building, is fluttering in his belly. Wayne's eyes fall upon Diane's shoulder bag that's on one of the bedside tables.

Is there a passport in the shoulder bag? Or maybe something else that might contribute to identity? If he were to go over and look through the bag he might find out. But what if Diane comes out of the bathroom and catches him? That could ruin everything. Or, what if she doesn't come out of the bathroom and he looks through her bag, but at some future time, later in the evening or the next day, she notices that things are different in her bag, for maybe she knows exactly how things are arranged and Wayne might not get that right in putting things back, so then she might accuse him of snooping, which would cause distrust and ill feeling. Or, she might notice he's gone through her bag, but she might not say anything. Wayne wouldn't know she knows that he's gone through her bag, which could be disadvantageous in any number of ways, for there could be repercussions, origins which he wouldn't understand. Given this reasoning, if he searched her bag, he'd be suspicious of Diane's behavior because she might know that he's gone through her bag but has chosen not to say anything.

Wayne sips his water while continuing to look at Diane's shoulder bag. It's made of leather and the leather is engraved with small triangles that run like a ribbon at the edges of the bag and its flap.

And what if he found a passport inside the bag and/or photographs in her wallet, for example, and discovers her identity, then what? Hey, you told me you're Diane, but actually you're Sally Smith from Fresno, California, and it seems you have a couple of kids. It also seems you're a police officer in Fresno . . . or a nurse or a firefighter or a taxi cab driver or . . . whatever. Okay, what then? Or what if Wayne found some discharge papers from a mental institution? There's no telling what kind of history he might find in that bag. And if he did find something, would it make things better between Diane and Wayne? As it is, things aren't bad right now. Also, it seems that things are going to get even better very soon.

EIGHT

Wayne turns back toward the window and looks down. A large man wearing a yellow shirt has just come out of the café. The man stops to talk to a man and a woman who are seated at a table with drinks and are smoking. The man gets out a pack of cigarettes from his shirt pocket and extracts a cigarette and puts it between his fat lips, and with this Wayne takes notice of the man's large head. The head and the yellow shirt—a shiver runs up Wayne's backbone. Wayne steps back from the window to assume a more discreet position, but doesn't give up watching the man. Light from inside the café radiates out through windows and the open doorway, and there are a few lights fastened to the exterior wall of the café for the benefit of those at outdoor tables.

There is a sound. The bathroom door is opening. Wayne turns. Diane comes out wearing one of her new dresses, fabric with puffs of white on light blue, images of clouds in a blue sky suggested. A subtle, yet glistening, red is on Diane's lips. Her hair too, very black, emits a sheen. She smiles in a shy way, eyes touching on Wayne but then averting. It is a new look, a look Wayne hasn't seen, a look that doesn't seem like Diane.

"Perhaps you could open that bottle of white wine, Wayne."

He steps over to the small refrigerator and he takes out a bottle of wine. Diane goes to her shoulder bag and Wayne thinks: Yes, she's checking to see if I've looked through it. But as he's handling the bottle and the corkscrew, he sees that Diane isn't scrutinizing the contents of the bag, for she simply pulls out a little paper bag and takes out a postcard. The little bag goes on the bedside table next to her shoulder bag. With Diane walking over to the writing desk that's been set up to look like a dining table, Wayne goes to work on the cork in the bottle. The room is modestly warm, window remaining open, curtains to the side.

As Wayne comes to the table with the opened bottle, Diane sets the postcard down on the table with a little snap that draws Wayne's eyes to the card— Claude Monet, *Poppies*, also known as *Poppy Field*, oil on canvas, 1873. Suddenly everything in the setting before Wayne's eyes becomes part of that painting, including Diane. Odd, because the two women in the painting, each with a child alongside, one woman-and-child at the top of a slope, the other near the bottom of the slope, have hats and dresses on that are formal in style. But still . . . perhaps it's the blue sky between white clouds or the red poppies on the slope or the evocation of a spring day that do the trick. But actually, it's the other way around, for on the table there are red poppies arranged languidly in a glass, and there's Diane's dress that's like the sky in Monet's painting.

Wayne looks at Diane, and again there's a bashful smile that paints her demeanor as if she were all so proper. The play between Monet's innocent picture and Diane is palpable.

"Do you remember this painting, Wayne?"

"Of course. At the Orsay."

"Yes. At the Orsay, and then in that little shop. Wasn't this one of the cards you were considering? A souvenir, a remembrance maybe?"

"How do you know I was thinking of buying that card at the museum shop?"

"The museum shop? Yes, in there too. But then we went into that little shop near the museum, you know, before we went to the café where you left me."

Wayne looks at her questionably. She smiles shyly.

"Aren't you going to pour the wine, Wayne?"

He pours the wine, and they each pick up a glass while still standing. The gentle sounds of a Parisian side street on a warm evening whisper from the open window.

"To fine art," Diane says.

They raise their glasses.

"Yes," Wayne enunciates. "To fine art."

They sip wine. Diane seems to be blushing, and for whatever reason this ignites the wine's flavor more noticeably in Wayne's mouth. When Wayne swallows he sees Diane's thin throat move and he knows she is swallowing too. Diane draws one of the chairs back and sits down. Wayne does the same. They begin eating while drinking.

"This is so delicious," Wayne remarks, "particularly the olives."

"I'm so glad you like it, Wayne."

Wayne looks at her with the idea of smiling, but when he sees Diane smiling he can only look at her, for her smile resembles her words, complimentary yet questionable. Is she staging something, and if so what is it? The food and the wine are really good, and Diane looks really good too.

"Fancy restaurants," says Diane, "like famous brand-name shops on wide avenues . . ." She raises a hand as if to say, who needs them?

Wayne can't help but to agree. "Yes," he says, "who needs them?"

Diane giggles as if tickled in a private place, and what is that place if not a vein of understanding that's being shared? Wayne feels like giggling too. He picks up the bottle of wine and pours, first her glass, then his.

A car horn sounds. Diane looks at the window, which is higher up from where the two of them are seated. Wayne sees Diane's face turn neutral, radiance diminishing. Probably all Diane can see is the room's light reflecting from half the window, the screened half of the window simply dark, or at best with a few stars, maybe even the moon. Wayne stands up and goes to the window and closes it and draws the curtains. He turns and smiles. The room is suddenly quiet and everything about it is now changed.

Diane breaks off a piece of cheese and puts it in her mouth and starts chewing. Wayne remains standing near the window. Looking at Diane, he can feel the sharpness of the cheese puckering the insides of his cheeks. Diane pauses in her chewing. Wayne, as if invited, steps over to the table and sits down.

Diane resumes chewing. Her mouth opens a bit and Wayne can hear the stickiness of the cheese. The air in the room is motionless and the light from the bedside lamp, the only lamp that's on, has a yellowish tint. Wayne and Diane sit within the glow of that tint.

Diane's mouth moves lazily. Remnants of cheese as a tart aftertaste has her tongue exploring crevices, or so it seems via Wayne's tongue that's exploring crevices in his mouth. Diane starts an expression and with this Wayne understands that he's been staring, which Diane understands too, for that's the expression invading her face. The scene seems to have been orchestrated, Diane wanting Wayne to watch.

Diane brings her wineglass to her lips. Wine drifts into her mouth with hardly a ripple. Her lips come together as the glass tilts away from her mouth. Setting the glass down on the table, she looks at Wayne and swallows.

Wayne reaches for his glass of wine. As his fingers enfold the glass, Diane picks up the postcard. Wayne doesn't bring the wineglass to his mouth because Diane is showing him the card, which he looks at.

"Claude Monet," says Diane, and even though it seems they've been talking about Monet, these are the first real words declaring the artist. They sit with this for a few elegant moments. Diane's pronunciation of "Claude Monet" is refined.

Wayne says, "But you didn't mention that shop before."

Diane tilts her head, a questioning pose.

"The little shop between the Orsay and the café," Wayne says.

"Yes. Well, I'm only bringing it up now because it's pertinent."

And even though he understands this, for the card and the scene before Wayne are collaborating, he says, "Pertinent?"

Diane half-smiles.

NINE

They return to eating, and like before everything Wayne puts in his mouth tastes great. But there is this sense that something is going to happen. Wayne chews his food while contemplating "impending," for that's what characterizes the moment. On further thought, though, he understands that "impending" has portrayed his time with Diane since they first met, only hours ago.

He can hold it in no longer. "What's going to happen, Diane?"

Her mouth is juggling an olive pit, but then her mouth stops. She discreetly deposits the seed in her hand. Her hand puts the seed on the side of her plate. She uses a paper napkin on her fingers and on her lips, tidily and daintily. Wayne watches with a sense of fascination.

Diane stands up and walks over to Wayne's cargo pants that are draped over a compact suitcase that has roller-wheels and a collapsible handle. At a side pocket on the pants she unzips a zipper and extracts a postcard. Returning to the table, she sets the card down on top of the Monet card. Wayne looks at the card. Diane sits down.

Gustave Courbet, *The Origin of the World*, 1866, oil on canvas.

The entire scene shifts. The table setting is now a picture of half-eaten food. Diane's dress now hangs idly from her shoulders, thin fabric manifesting. The light from the lamp is now sepia. The scent of the room has a slight cheese smell, warm and a little damp.

Diane picks up a green olive and puts it in her mouth. Wayne's view has moved from the postcard to Diane's face. He watches as she shreds the olive of its oily meat while keeping her mouth closed, cheeks and jaw muscles working. The image on the postcard is in Wayne's mind, and yet the image of Diane working the olive in her mouth is also in his mind. It seems a contradiction, and so he wonders if his mind is flickering back and forth between the two images even though it is Diane's face that his eyes behold. Again, Diane rids her mouth of the olive pit in the same manner as before, or so it seems at first, for the mechanics are identical but this time instead of graceful there is nonchalance, as in languid. Perhaps she has come down a peg. Or maybe she has stepped sideways to allow another dimension.

Diane must have put that card in the pocket of his pants while he was taking a shower. But does he want to bring this up? After all, it would imply subterfuge.

"Do you remember this painting in the Orsay, Wayne?"

"Of course. Who could forget this painting?"

"Precisely. Who could forget this painting? You stood in front of it for a while, like so many people do.

But you couldn't stand there looking for too long, could you? For this piece presents a predicament for all its viewers. It hangs in one of the most prestigious museums in the world, for it is art. Yet even now it creates controversy. Realism doesn't excuse its statement. And neither does its title, which is almost a joke. But on the other hand, it's not a joke. Like all good art, this painting does not remain still. It moves amongst such terms as: erotic, vulgar, truthful, pornographic, exciting, disgusting. People don't want to be shy. They want to be open-minded, so they look at it. But they can't look at it for too long because that might imply something else. But the odd thing is, if you look at it for an extended time nothing happens. It becomes a painting. But a painting is a picture, and the picture is in the mind, which is where something can happen, depending on the person."

The way Diane now reaches for her glass of wine is part of the new scene, which her soliloquy has furthered. And the way Wayne picks up his glass of wine is part of the new scene too, for Diane has willed it. After they have taken a sip of wine, it is all so predictable that something will need to be said, and this is what Wayne thinks about as that dry white wine dwells in his mouth. They swallow and set their glasses down.

"You passed up any number of cards in that little shop. And why not? They had quite a selection. Probably everything that's housed in the Orsay. But," says Diane, "you purchased this card." She nods to indicate the Courbet card.

Wayne is about to speak, but Diane, as if anticipating this, resumes speaking before he can begin.

"I thought it was rather daring of you, to walk up to

that little old lady who was in back of the counter, and then to purchase this one card, no others. A single purchase. Of course it was cheap."

Diane smiles and it's like she is on the verge of giggling. She is pleased and amused.

"What do you think that little old lady was thinking, Wayne?"

"I have no idea."

"I'll tell you what she was thinking. She was thinking nothing. These issues concerning this painting are no longer of any relevance to her. She has moved on. Her realities are different from what they were years ago. She was simply selling a postcard."

Wayne nods in agreement.

"But for you, it was more than a postcard," Diane says. "And for me, while standing at a rack of cards and looking on, it was more than a man simply buying a postcard."

The room is stark still. Diane stands up and steps over to the bed, bedspread a patchwork quilt in pastels. Diane hikes up her dress to her belly, no undergarments, and lies down on the bed, head resting on the bulge from a pillow under the bedspread.

She looks over at Wayne who is looking at her, and what Wayne sees is an exact likeness of the Courbet painting. What has been anticipated is now being realized, and what is being realized is what Wayne has been seeking, yet there was nothing in its making that was foreknown.

Diane smiles slowly, her mouth in some sort of awaiting contortion.

TEN

Her dress is on the floor next to the bed and his *yukata* is next to her dress. They are like their discarded garments, but they are on the bed, resplendent in the afterglow of copulation. The room has returned to sepia and silent, whereas minutes before it was something else, for Diane was vocal and sepia was lit up with embers.

"We are lovers," Diane whispers.

Wayne is looking up at the ceiling. Diane's head lies in the crook of his arm. "We are lovers" teases his ears, but then errant thoughts have him wondering about foreplay. Did it begin with the Courbet postcard? Or did it begin with that dramatic kiss on that side street after they left the park? Or maybe it was in the park itself. The escapade at the pharmacy with the condoms also comes to mind.

"We have history now," Diane tells him, her voice dreamy.

"History," Wayne says, half question, half statement.

"Yes. Something to build on. Something to refer to."

There's a different voice now and it hints at tantalizing. There is also a whiff of nostalgia invading that voice.

"You were so cute in that shop where you bought the pornographic postcard," Diane relates and chuckles. Wayne, too, chuckles even though he doubts the content of Diane's observation.

"You were trying to pass it off as art, weren't you?"

"I suppose so," Wayne answers.

Diane rises, leaving Wayne's arm on the bedspread. She looks at Wayne's naked body before swinging her legs over the side of the bed to stand up. Wayne's eyes go to the side. He can see Diane from the bellybutton up. Her flesh is soft in the yellowish light from the lamp. She goes to the table and pours wine into one of the stemmed glasses. Stepping over to the window with the wineglass in hand, she shoves the curtains to the side and slides the window open with her free hand. Immediately there are sounds from the street and from the city in general. Soon after this there is night air entering the room. While looking out the window, Diane sips wine. Wayne watches her, his head elevated on the hump from the pillow. Diane seems absorbed, like maybe the city is talking to her and maybe she is listening.

She turns in a picturesque manner, completely naked, and she says: "Let us go out into the night, for this is Paris!"

Downstairs on the sidewalk, Diane looks across the street. Perhaps she's searching for the man with the big head and yellow shirt, but he's nowhere in sight.

Diane's wearing the other dress she purchased at the boutique, a long-sleeved one-piece that comes to her knees, beige in color but darkened with little lavender flowers the size of dimes. The red beret is atop her head, huaraches on her feet. She wears the dark vest with the red stitching. It is not really cool out, much less cold, but there is a suggestion of coolness. Moisture is in the air, perhaps from the river nearby. Wayne, too, is in long sleeves, a plaid flannel shirt, and from the waist down cargo pants.

They turn left and begin walking. People are on the streets and in cafés. It is Friday night. They come to the Pont de l'Alma Bridge but they don't cross it. Instead they go right and walk along Quai d'Orsay, which parallels the Seine. Diane slips her arm through Wayne's and they stroll as couple. The lights on the opposite bank are dazzling and doubly so because they reflect off the river. Boats cruise the water slowly. Some of the boats are very long and they carry tourists. At the Invalides, which is luminous, they mount the Pont Alexandre III Bridge, a monument of beauty. They start across the bridge on its walkway, cars moving to their right.

Pedestrians are frequent but the walkway isn't crowded, so it's easy to walk arm-in-arm. Halfway across the bridge they stop to gaze at the water below and it's then that Diane stiffens. She jerks her head up and starts pulling Wayne by the arm. She is trying to run. Wayne starts trotting alongside her, his head twisting this way and that in an effort to locate the threat. Perhaps the man with the big head is in back of them. Diane, letting go of Wayne's arm, runs all out, Right Bank her destination.

"What is it?" Wayne yells as he starts running too,

both of them dodging pedestrians in their flight. "What is it?"

"The river! It's coming out of the river!"

"What?" Wayne shouts.

Diane doesn't answer. Not even when they're off the bridge and walking at a clip does she say anything, and neither does she look back. At Champs-Elysees they stop, a marvelous boulevard in either direction. Diane is gaining her breath and so is Wayne. Diane looks over her shoulder.

"We're safe here," she says. "It's not following us."

"What?"

"Didn't you see it? That malevolent being."

"No."

She looks at Wayne sharply and Wayne looks back at her and he sees a red beret outlined with shiny black hair that frames a white face, lips red, eyes extravagant. The boulevard is sparkling and it's that light that's on Diane's face.

"It was coming out of the river! My God, didn't you see it?"

Wayne almost says no, thought and utterance forming, but he holds back because of Diane, who is stunning, yet frightful. She is calming down, though, and yet . . . Wayne gives a timid chuckle. Diane looks at this and laughs too.

"We have escaped with our lives, Wayne. How joyous!"

She takes Wayne's arm and they walk to the right. They come to a café with outdoor seating and sit down at a table. A waiter arrives promptly and Diane orders. When the waiter returns he sets four small cups that are on small saucers down on the table along with glasses of water. Diane has ordered four espresso coffees. The waiter gives a brief smile as if appreciating the simplicity of the order. He departs gracefully.

"What a lovely night," Diane says.

Wayne has to agree. "Yes," he says.

Diane picks up one of the small white cups and sips. Wayne follows suit. The coffee is strong and rich, and it does its trick, yet that trick was already in motion with the events on the bridge. Wayne is awake. The effects of the alcohol he consumed early are gone.

ELEVEN

They leave the café and they come to Place de la Concorde with its Egyptian obelisk. A little farther on they descend into a Metro station where they board a train. They are not long on the train. When they disembark, Wayne sees a sign: *Abbesses*. It was at the previous stop, though, that most of the people got off the train: *Pigalle*. Abbesses is evidently a deep station, for they take an elevator and ascend. Wayne is vaguely aware of where they are, but "vaguely" is soon swept away when Diane says: "Montmartre, 18th arrondissement."

Wayne looks around. People are about, but it's not crowded.

"We skipped the garish crowds," Diane informs him. "Pigalle and the sex shops."

They begin walking. Sacré-Coeur can be seen clearly, for it is lit up and sits just above them. From the Metro station they progress to the right in a general way, traversing a slope laterally, and Wayne reflects how a part of Diane's backstory is hinted at, for she seems to know the neighborhood. It isn't long before they arrive at Square Louise Michel where they join a modest crowd ascending steps that lead to the church at the top of the hill, the highest point in Paris. People are mostly quiet, footsteps the dominate sound. It's like a pilgrimage in the night. Of course people are descending, but it is the trudging shoes laboring on the incline that portend reverence. The faithful are paying homage. Wayne looks at Diane—red beret, black vest, white face. She is eager like a child.

As with everyone else, they arrive at a flat area in front of the church, and it is there that they look out at Paris, a vista that goes on and on until it fades into mist. Wayne's eyes locates landmarks, first of which is the Eiffel Tower, sparkling goldish. Diane has her arm through Wayne's. Other couples, too, are like that. People talk in murmurs as if cooing.

When that spectacular view is finally exhausted, they turn to view a white edifice, looming and illuminated. They enter the church, which is no less magnificent inside than outside, but it's a different magnificence. It surrounds them, just as it surrounds each and every visitor who enters its embrace. People move in awe, tourism left behind. The church's interior tells Wayne why basilica is part of its naming: The Basilica of the Sacred Heart of Paris – Sacré-Coeur Basilica. The exterior of the church does not describe the architectural design of a basilica, but the inside does—oblong, prominent nave, high alter with an apse in back, vaulted ceiling. There is stained glass and there are exquisite mosaics that weave art and religion.

"Let us pray," Diane says.

"Pray?"

"Yes."

They walk up an aisle. Diane stops and genuflects and slips into a pew where she kneels down on a kneeler and places her forearms on top of the back of the pew in front. Wayne does the same, thus kneeling next to Diane. Diane makes the sign of the cross and brings her hands together and intertwines her fingers. Wayne imitates this. The church is quiet.

Wayne doesn't know how to pray, so he wonders how Diane does. As far as he can tell, there is nothing but silence from Diane. Wayne decides to copy this, and so they kneel without a word or a whisper while facing the focal point of the basilica where a dazzling mosaic glints.

Diane makes the sign of the cross, forehead, upper stomach, left and right side of her chest, and then brings her hands together briefly. She comes off the kneeler to slide back on the pew's seat and rest her back against the wooden back of the pew. Wayne does the same.

After a few moments, Wayne turns to Diane and whispers: "What did we pray for?"

Diane accepts this without surprise, and says: "We prayed for happiness."

They sit with the wonders of that magnificent architecture around them as if its splendors were a call to belief.

TWELVE

Diane rises and so does Wayne. They step into the aisle, where they genuflect. They turn and walk toward the rear of the church, which is where they exit into the night that hasn't changed since they left it. But maybe they have changed, which is what Wayne thinks about as they look out at Paris again from that hilltop where a white church resides like statuary lifted from Istanbul, for the church's exterritorial architecture is more Eastern than Western.

Diane leads the way down the steps and then into narrow streets that wind this way and that on a hillside that constitutes Montmartre, cobblestone surfaces common, but does Diane know where she is going?

They stop in front of a wooden door that has the sounds of a piano in back of it, not loud, but comprehensible. Diane tilts her head as if to listen with one ear, red beret at an angle, black hair around the beret reflecting what is emitted from a meek lightbulb that's at the end of a curved rod above the door.

"It is Satie," Diane utters in a low voice. "Gymno-pedie Number One."

Diane's face shifts, ocher light from that struggling filament creating pockets of shadow on her visage. Wayne pulls the door open as if instructed, but there's been no issuance of instructions. They breach the threshold of that cryptic doorway and enter. The room, as expected, is not brightly lit. Wayne closes the door.

The tune from the piano isn't loud. It's shy, yet it dominates the room. People are at tables, and of tables there is one which is particularly long with groups of three or four people sitting along its length on either side. The piano, an upright, is against a wall to the left. The room continues around in a short L-shape to Wayne's right, which is the direction Diane starts for. Two vacant tables are in that space. Diane and Wayne sit down. The table is wooden and so are the chairs. Floorboard run with groves from wear and age. A waitress comes to their table in an unobtrusive nonchalance as to not disturb the music. Satie continues.

The waitress, in common everyday clothing, doesn't say anything. She simply stands, her hair black and with streaks of gray like silver thread, and already she has wrinkles. Her glasses seem to be bifocals in the way she works her head to look at Wayne and Diane. Diane orders softly and the waitress understands instantly.

The piano man, stringy hair falling to his shoulders, is long and slim. His profile occupies Wayne's view. Beige light is on the man's ashen face. His fingers move like liquid on the keys of the piano. In his expression there is something that suggests a dream.

Looking toward the bar, which has several high stools with nobody on them, Wayne sees a sight taken from an old movie, barman aged, hands large, knuckles protruding. A couple of glasses have light green liquid in their bottom halves. A spoon-like utensil is perched across the rim of each glass, with a cube of white sugar crumbling on each utensil. The barman is dripping water from a glass pitcher alternately over one cube and then the other, green liquid in the bottom half of the glass turning milky, yet retaining a green tint, while rising proportionately to the dripping water.

"Absinthe," Wayne says to Diane, who flashes a conspiratorial expression.

Wayne's eyes investigate the audience. It is not a young crowd. It is a relaxed crowd, a respectful crowd, a crowd used to the effects of alcohol. They've been here before. Pieces of cheese and broken bread are on plates.

When their greenish drinks arrive via the waitress, Wayne and Diane look at those hourglass-shaped glasses as they sit on the wooden table before their eyes. With nothing else left to do, they pick the glasses up and sip. A strange concoction of licorice and sweetness results, breath of those spirits siphoning up through sinuses, and still that lamenting piano continues, memory of a drizzly night prevailing, cobblestones glistening in a damp reflection. Change infects Diane's face. Are there now crow's feet at the edges of her wilting eyes? The beret isn't so red. It's amber, as is her complexion, but of course the lighting might account for this, but then there's the turn of her mouth which has a plaintive proportion. Wayne feels the same way, but it isn't sadness. It's aloneness, caused by the world's indifference.

The piano man's fingers fade to an ending that leaves lingering notes. A ruffle of applause builds until there is only applause. He gets up from the piano bench and walks over to the bar. A few people approach the piano to shove euro notes into a glass that's on top of the upright. Wayne, too, goes to the piano to stick some money into the glass.

Diane and Wayne resume with their drinks. Sweetness oozes, a clinging quality. Diane stands up and goes to the end of the bar that's closest to their table, which is where a rack of postcards sit. She turns the rack and looks at the cards. The barman and pianist are in conversation a few feet away, pianist with a glass of red wine. A friendly exchange of words develops between the barman and the pianist and Diane. Perhaps her selection of a card instigates this, for she has lifted a card from its slot and is showing it to the barman and pianist. Diane walks back to where Wayne is sitting. She sets the card on the table for Wayne's eyes. She sits down, her chair next to Wayne's.

"Edgar Degas, *L'Absinthe*. It hangs in the Orsay, Wayne."

He looks at the card. The man and woman in the painting are not Wayne and Diane, and yet the man and woman sit at a wooden table with another wooden table alongside, a café scene, drinks on the table, woman dazed, man no better. Wayne looks at Diane. She kind of smiles.

The piano man comes to their table, holding his glass of wine. He seems friendly. His pants are black and they are wrinkled. His shirt is white, long-sleeved. He looks down at the Degas postcard.

"Would you care to have a seat?" Wayne says and gestures to the chair opposite himself and Diane. The man smiles, teeth dim.

He says, "Thank you," and sits down.

"How did you know I speak English?" the man asks.

"I didn't. It's just that it's the only language I speak," Wayne answers.

The man smiles anew. He seems to appreciate Wayne's honesty.

"The lady speaks fluent French," the man says and indicates Diane. "Where are you from?" the pianist asks.

But before Wayne can reply, Diane says, "Your piano playing is wonderful. Do you play here regularly?"

"Yes. Three nights a week."

A scratchy sound begins from a couple of speakers, and then there's a soft trumpet. A vinyl disc is obviously turning under a needle, yesteryear technology adding to the room's ambiance. The three of them sit, listening.

"Chet Baker," Wayne asserts.

The pianist gets out a pack of Gauloises. He shakes the pack and a cigarette comes a quarter of the way out. He first offers this to Wayne, who declines, and then to Diane, who declines as well.

The trumpet continues, all so soft, a bass backing it. Other instruments come in, a sax and drums. But that's it. A small combo, and yet so complete. The tune is like a melancholy lullaby.

The pack of Gauloises, a short pack, cigarettes unfiltered, remains in the piano man's hand. He seems to have forgotten about it.

"It's so much better than when he sang this," the piano man says, a British accent about his speech, which is slow and soft, like the music and like the room.

"*My Funny Valentine*," the piano man continues. "Chet really knew how to do this, just with the horn."

Both Diane and Wayne are looking at the piano man, whose cheeks are drawn, and whose complexion is blotted with gray and black whiskers, a two-day growth.

"He was popular here, you know, in Paris, in Europe."

It sounds like the piano man knew Baker. Wayne would like to ask about this, but that would be a question relating to past.

"Too bad we don't have some heroin," Diane says.

The piano man looks at Diane's face. Diane accepts this. Wayne looks at her, too.

The tune draws to an end. The piano man looks down at his pack of cigarettes and then glances around the room. Someone is paying their bill at the bar.

"I better go outside," the piano man says and stands up, but not abruptly. He looks at Wayne and Diane and he kind of grins. Diane and Wayne smile back. The piano man, glass of wine in hand, makes for the door, where he follows a group of three outside. The next piece on the album starts, a livelier tune, but still, there's that Baker softness.

They sip from their glasses. They look at the postcard. They listen to music coming from an old record.

"I could never have had a Paris like this without you," Wayne says.

Diane smiles.

THIRTEEN

They finish their drinks and Wayne goes to the bar to pay the bill. Outside, the piano man is standing, a short length of cigarette smolder between his fingers, glass of wine in the other hand. Diane and Wayne stop to acknowledge him. They stand for a moment, the three of them.

"I'll take that cigarette now if you're still offering," Diane says.

"Oh, sure."

The piano man drops the butt of his cigarette on the ground to free his one hand, which he uses to get the pack of Gauloises out of his shirt pocket. He shakes a cigarette out of the pack for Diane to take. He then looks at Wayne. Wayne indicates, "No thanks."

The piano man puts the pack back where it came from and from the same pocket takes out a lighter. He flicks a small wheel and a flame appears. Diane leans forward with the cigarette in her mouth and the piano man lights the cigarette. Diane draws deeply after an initial puff. The night is a little cool now. Smoke lazily creeps out of Diane's mouth on the exhale. The piano man brings his glass of wine up and sips. It's a thick, squat glass, wide bevels running vertically. The piano man rubs the bottom of his shoe on the smoldering cigarette butt that's on the ground.

"It is a lovely evening," Diane says.

"Indeed it is," the piano man answers.

"A black-and-white movie," Diane remarks, voice smoky.

The piano man looks at her.

Diane inhales again, and when she exhales there is smoke not only from her mouth but from the nostrils of her nose as well. Both Wayne and the piano man watch this. Diane looks down at the cigarette that she holds in her fingers European style.

"Well, I better get back inside and play some more music."

The piano man gives Wayne and Diane a good-bye glance and opens the door and steps through that opening like a departing character from a departed age. He pulls the door closed in back of himself.

***

Wayne and Diane walk in a general downhill direction. They come to a stairway with steel handrails and they descend. A nimble woman, hair bouncing, is trotting up the concrete steps, brisk sounds coming from her shoes as the soles hit one step and then the next in quick succession. She doesn't look at Wayne or Diane, but Wayne and Diane look at her.

"She is going to her lover," Diane claims, while stopping at a landing to look back at the woman who continues uphill on the stairs. "She has gotten off work at a café and she's in a hurry."

Wayne, standing on the concrete landing next to

Diane, looks back at the woman too, who disappears from sight at the top of the stairs.

Diane remarks, "She can hardly wait."

Turning and looking out at Paris from that landing exposes a city that's taking on mist. Diane inhales and her cigarette flares red. They leave the landing to follow an alley-like street. Blackened blocks of stone, smeared by weather, line the byway and rise up as the walls of two-story residences. Every so often there's a door or a gate or a window, and it is the occasional window that provides the alleyway with light. What is the point of taking this route is a question that is answered when Diane stops to put her back against a dank wall, while issuing instructions.

"Put your hand up my dress," she rasps. "Hurry."

Wayne's hand goes to the bottom hem of Diane's dress and trails up her leg to find no undergarments, fingers falling into a warm crevice. Diane responds by thrusting a hip out, and then there's her lifting the cigarette to her mouth and inhaling. Wayne looks at her eyes and sees only blackness with a glint. When Diane exhales it comes with touches of a moan and the smoke seems jerky as it catches in a flick of light. From somewhere down the way, in the direction of their supposed route, sounds of a stubborn hinge creak, but no one appears in that direction nor in any other. The red glow of the cigarette falls to the ground. Diane's hand goes to Wayne's shoulder for support as she trembles.

There's some sort of signal from Diane's body, as if it's had enough. Wayne withdraws his hand. A pause, and then they resume walking, cigarette left to die on the rounded bricks that pave the lane. The sounds of Diane's huaraches on those selfsame bricks are the only sounds in a poignant night until a TV is heard in back of a curtained window.

They enter a street that's on a sharp incline. A motorcycle is coming up the slope, headlight staccato on the pavement. Diane grabs Wayne by the upper arm and together they shove into an indent where a wrought iron gate resides. Diane has Wayne and herself against the inner corner of that shallow alcove.

When the motorcycle passes with a rumble Diane and Wayne peek out to watch it. The headlights of a small car coming downhill dismiss the motorcycle. The car soon passes by and with this its identity is understood, an old Citron, tinny and loose.

Diane looks up and down the street that is now vacant and she says, "That might have been the Gestapo."

"Which one," asks Wayne, "the car or the bike?"

They emerge from that indentation of an alcove, graffiti-scripted wall on either side. The neighborhood speaks of middle-class wealth. They resume a cautions route downward, Wayne's question left unanswered.

Traffic appears at a cross street, pedestrians too, and when they reach that activity with its illumination they turn left and walk on a comfortable sidewalk. In the middle of the street, dividing traffic, is a park that runs along the length of the street. At a dissecting street that runs uphill they look to their left, which gives them a clear view of Sacré-Coeur as it sits in its blonde splendor.

FOURTEEN

Diane motions, finger coming to her lips to indicate that it's time for a glass of wine, and so they steer into a café all so easily. The place is lively with customers. They choose to stand at the bar where service is immediate. Two stemmed glasses with red wine are set down in front of them. They pick up their respective glasses and pause as if to toast to something, whatever that might be.

"We made it," Diane alleges, "despite the curfew."

And this is what they toast to.

A framed poster advertising the Moulin Rouge hangs on one of the walls. It is a reproduction of Toulouse-Lautrec's work.

Diane gestures with her glass and says to Wayne, "You remember Lautrec from the Orsay, don't you? A number of paintings, *Rousse* of particular interest, also called *Toilet*."

A man and a woman standing next to them seem to have taken an interest in what Diane is saying. Both the man and the woman are heavyset. Perhaps it is the language, English, that has attracted their interest.

"The Moulin Rouge?" the man says. "We just came from there."

"You don't say," Diane chimes. "And did you and the Mrs. take in the show?"

"We certainly did," the man says with a broad smile, clean-shaven face reddish, a hue that the woman next to him shares on her corpulent phizzog. "And we had a bottle of champagne and a little something to eat as well." The man's English is North American.

"How splendid," Diane remarks.

"Yes," says the woman next to the man. "And isn't it funny that we should stop here for a drink and find a Lautrec poster of the Moulin Rouge on the wall?"

"Yes," Diane says.

"And that you should mention the Orsay," the woman continues, "for we were there this morning."

"No kidding," Diane enthuses.

"Yes," the woman gushes. "We love Paris. We've been here twice before, and not just for one of those overnight tour stops. We always stay for four nights and for four eventful days, but this is the first time we've been to the Moulin Rouge. Can you imagine— the Moulin Rouge! And champagne no less!"

"Oh, it must have been marvelous!" Diane reports back.

"It was."

"And look at these," the man says while pulling a stack of postcards out of the pocket of his sports coat. He sets the cards down on the bar. "Keepsakes from the museum shop at the Orsay."

"Well, I'll be," Diane affirms while looking down at the cards.

The man proceeds to turn over one card at a time slowly, one famous painting after the next, which has the attention of the four of them. The man pauses to sip red wine, and so the others sip from their glasses as well. But then Diane looks toward the door of the café and her face goes gloom. She grabs Wayne's forearm, fingers digging in.

"He's a collaborator," Diane hisses, which causes the man and his wife to look. Wayne looks too.

"A collaborator?" the man questions while looking at a man who's going out the doors of the café, a slim man with the collar of his herringbone sports jacket flipped up to around his neck.

"With the occupational forces, who else?" Diane says.

The man in question walks through the outdoor seating area to turn left and disappear along the sidewalk.

"Occupational forces?" the woman questions.

The three of them are looking at Diane, and what they see is a face returning to jovial, although she remarks, "I'm glad he's gone."

And it's left at that, the four of them raising their glasses and sipping.

* * *

Diane's eyes return to the stack of postcards, which serves to direct everyone else's eyes to the cards, and so the man starts turning them over again one at a time. The fourth card he comes to is Gustave Courbet's *The Origin of the World*, vagina and pubic hair in vivid display. A pause is shared by the four of them as they look at the card.

"How did that get in there?" the man says. "I didn't buy this."

The denial draws more attention to the picture. The man turns the card over, and so it takes its place atop the other cards that have been turned over, but then the woman says, "Are you going to keep that, Corky?"

"Of course not. I'm not going to keep it," the man replies and turns the card back over so that its front side is up, stunning realism renewed, which in turn renews the dilemma of what to do with the card. Corky picks the card up and shreds it vigorously into little pieces. The little pieces become a pile of debris on the surface of the bar.

Corky's wife and Diane and Wayne have watched Corky's treatment of the card. In the wake of this there is another gap that has the four of them hoisting their wineglasses. The card that's face-up on the stack of to-be-viewed cards is Claude Monet's *The Magpie*, a snowy, wintery scene.

As if to relieve an assumed tension, Diane says, "We spent the evening praying in a church. We thought it would be safer to go to a church as opposed to a synagogue. And besides, it's the same God, isn't it?"

Corky and the Mrs. look at Diane. Diane blinks her eyes, a shy gesture, and yet she seems to be basking in the attention she has drawn. Wayne, too, displays a keen interest in what Diane has said, and in what she might say next, but it is the woman, Corky's partner, who contributes next.

"Praying? How nice. And on a Friday night no less when everyone is out partying." She smiles, red lipstick a little weak on her puffy lips. It's been a long evening.

"You must be devout . . ." Corky begins, but trails off because there's the question of devout what?

Coming to Corky's aid, Diane says, "We were praying for our daughter who's at Drancy."

"Drancy?" questions the Mrs. "Is that faraway?"

"Of course not. It's in the suburbs here, north-eastern sector."

"Oh. Well . . ." The woman leaves what she began hanging.

"She could be going east soon," Diane says.

"East?" says Corky. "You mean she's leaving, going to take a trip? And you were . . . praying for her safe journey? Where exactly is she going?"

"Poland."

"Poland," enunciates Corky, "is nice during the summer. Winters, though, are a different story. We haven't actually been there, Marsha and I, but friends have told us. It's also supposed to be very cheap."

Diane looks at Corky and then at Marsha. Both Corky and Marsha are smiling.

"A vacation?" Corky suggests. "Or is it a business trip? Is she going there to work?"

Diane picks up her wineglass as if she needs something to calm her nerves. She sips. She sets her glass down and looks at Corky.

"That's what they're told—work. But everyone knows what this is," Diane says.

Corky shifts his weight. Marsha, too, seems uneasy.

Diane gestures in the direction of Wayne's wineglass. Wayne picks the glass up and drains it. Diane's glass is already empty.

"It is time we should be leaving," Diane says.

"Oh, yes," says Corky. "Well, it was nice talking with you. Have a wonderful time in Paris!"

Diane gives Corky a look. Corky is smiling, teeth widely gapped. Diane looks at Marsha. She, too, is smiling. Diane turns and starts for the open doorway. Wayne follows.

FIFTEEN

They can't enter the cathedral because it's closed at this hour. Diane, though, doesn't exhibit any disappointment. Not that she isn't interested in the church, for she is, and it's this interest that Wayne notes because Diane is leaning right and left, tilting her head up and down as she looks at the front of the church. Her face and body express attentiveness, and it hits Wayne that this is exactly what she has shown in all the camellia-like personalities she has assumed and impersonated in Wayne's presence. Diane totally inhibits whatever she's involved with. Multiple personalities or phobias come to mind, but these terms are too tidy. Diane cannot be packaged into something like a nutcase. If she could, Wayne wouldn't be at her side searching the exterior of Notre Dame for . . . "the Hunchback."

A spacious area is before the cathedral and it is in this area that they stand along with a few other people. The church is lit up, as are other notable buildings along the Seine. Gargoyles peek out from the cathedral's elaborate edifice.

"Can you see him?" Diane asks.

"No," Wayne answers.

"Let's move over this way," Diane says. "Maybe we can get a glimpse of him from over there."

They move to their right, which puts them closer to the river, but of course Notre Dame sits on an island in the Seine, so left or right would put them closer to the river, yet it is to their right, as they look at the cathedral, that the river is the closest, cathedral set back from that bank with nothing in between, and if they were to cross the Seine via a nearby bridge, it would be that branch of the river that would reflect the lighted church.

"I still can't see him," Diane says.

"No, neither can I," Wayne replies.

They are craning their necks.

"He must be in one of those cavities or maybe in the bell tower feeding sugar plums to his girlfriend," Diane says. "If I could only put my eyes on him it would excite me so much."

Close by a young couple is taking a selfie. Diane walks over. Wayne walks over too.

"Hello there," Diane says. "Did you by any chance see Quasimodo? Or better yet, take a picture of him?"

The man is lowering a selfie stick, photo having been taken. A trim beard enhances his face. The young woman next to the man smiles in a questioning way at Diane. The woman is wearing a petite blue jacket, leather perhaps. The man says something in French. Diane responds back in French. The man and woman explode in laughter. Diane laughs too, and so Wayne laughs. The four of them are laughing.

"They think I'm joking," Diane says to Wayne in English, but Diane hasn't taken offense. Just the opposite. She is cheerful.

More French is exchanged. More laughter occurs. The young couple strolls away in merriment and in love.

"Aren't they cute," Diane remarks. Wayne smiles.

"The Hunchback," Diane resumes. "Hunched over with his arms hanging down."

Wayne bends in a hunching manner, arms dangling. He twists his head to look at Diane sideways and he screws up his face, one end of his mouth downward.

"That's it!" Diane exclaims.

Wayne moves crablike, feet in stutters, knees buckled, one eye thrust upward looking at Diane. Diane squeals. Wayne grunts.

"I want you like that," Diane says. "When we get back to the room, we'll be in the bell tower, and I'll be on my hands and knees in front of the full-length mirror and you'll be in back of me. I'll see you in the mirror and you'll be drooling and groaning."

They use a nearby bridge to cross the Seine, which puts them in the vicinity of a bookshop that Diane gravitates to in all seriousness. The bookstore is closed, interior dark, no one around, area in front of the shop quiet. Diane and Wayne stand before the shop's muted hominess in awe.

Diane pronounces, "The English-language bookstore."

"Yes," Wayne replies.

From a pocket of her dress Diane withdraws the academic glasses she purchased at the knickknacks store, frames round and made of faded yellow plastic, lenses plain glass. She sets those spectacles on her face carefully. Wayne watches. There is enough nearby light to see Diane clearly. The red beret and the short black hair framing the hat, and then those circles of yellowish plastic and their reflective lenses, Diane stands serenely, studying the world.

"Joyce," Wayne announces.

They move on, arm-in-arm, glasses remaining on Diane's face. They wander away from the Seine. They venture into the Latin Quarter.

"We must have whiskey," Diane states.

They enter a café that is moderately busy. They sit at a table. A waiter arrives. Diane orders. Four glasses are delivered via a silver tray, two glasses with water and two glasses with two inches of amber liquid that betrays whiskey. They pick up the amber-liquid glasses and pause.

"If I only had an Irish lilt," Diane says.

They sip, taste smooth, aroma pungent. Framed reproductions alluding to modernism are on the walls, photographs and paintings. Diane directs Wayne's attention to a colorful piece where Divisionism is at work.

"Do you remember it from the Orsay?" Diane asks.

"Matisse, *Luxury, Calm and Pleasure*," Wayne responds.

"Yes, that'd be the English title. Some say it was the first stirrings of Fauvism."

More whiskey in little sips, and then water.

"The Steins live in this quarter," Diane tells Wayne.

"Live?"

"Well . . . At any rate, farther away from the river than where we are now, but in the Latin Quarter. Everyone knows Gertrude, but it's actually Sarah, who's married to Michael, Gertrude's brother, who has an eye for Matisse. Matisse's studio is on quay St. Michel, very nearby."

Diane pauses.

"Can you feel it, Wayne?"

"I think so."

Diane motions, which brings the waiter. Words are exchanged. Both Diane and the waiter seem pleased, smiles and quick responses. Whatever it is has been settled, for the waiter walks off with a jaunt.

"We're in luck," Diane informs Wayne. "They have leftover chicken from the dinner menu, chicken with rosemary. We'll be dining."

"Good. I'm hungry."

SIXTEEN

They finish their whiskeys. The chicken is delivered, olive oil and sprigs of rosemary dripping over it, a basket of bread accompanying. Utensils and cloth napkins are set down. A word or two between Diane and the waiter, who then goes away and returns with two glasses of white wine. They begin eating, bustle of the café surrounding them. Diane looks so European with her red beret and round-lensed glasses and her handling of a knife and fork.

She says, "Impressionism, Post-Impressionism, Modernism. But we mustn't forget Realism, which in the case of literature can be attributed to Flaubert, and would Modernism have been possible without Realism?"

Wayne stops eating to look at her.

"We are having a serious discussion, Wayne."

"I guess we are."

"And then there's Beckett. Some say his work is the end of Modernism. Others claim it's the beginning of Post-Modernism. He writes in French, you know.

Afterwards he translates it into English. For the most part, he makes his home in France, spends a great deal of time in Paris. His adult life, I'm talking about. As for his childhood and education, like Joyce—Ireland."

They return to their food, which they attack as if were essential.

Diane waves her fork while chewing. Clearing space in her mouth for words, she says, "Writers, painters, sculptors, musicians, composures, and terrible weather."

"And the occupation," adds Wayne in recalling what Diane has invented or believes.

Diane stops everything to look at Wayne. She sets her knife and fork down, click, weighty utensils finding comfort on a slick of olive oil, chicken having been dispensed with. Wayne is using a piece of bread to soak up the rosemary-flavored oil on his plate. He sticks the bread in his mouth and chews, and in this he seems oblivious to Diane, but as her eyes dart right and left Wayne stops chewing. She leans forward across the table and whispers: "We must be careful."

Wayne sees fear on Diane's face.

"We should be leaving," Diane says.

Wayne leaves money on the table and they depart.

The night has grown late and the side streets they navigate are mostly vacant, passageways extracted from black-and-white cinema, one street bending into the next like montage, shoes on cobblestone a sound-track. Mist has set in. They huddle side-by-side while slipping between buildings—a stray cat, a dripping faucet, a row of battered trashcans. They emerge onto a wider avenue—a few passing cars, pedestrians on occasion, a lone café on a diminutive corner. Where a modest window is lit with a small light that illuminates a framed canvas no larger than a foot and a half square, they stop.

Oil undoubtedly, paint thick in places, brushstrokes flagrant, yet not unduly so, for the painting is bold but not pretentious. There is subject, thus it is not purely abstract, but by no means is it blatant realism. It rests on a miniature easel, and it is bordered with a tawny-colored frame made of wood, but then there is a larger frame, which is the window, and the window is that of a small gallery. The single little light, coned in a funnel of tin, is directed only at the painting, which leaves the rest of the window space dark. It is only through a door to the right that houses paned glasses that a peek into the shop is possible, but not much can be seen, only the outlines of frames.

The focal point of the painting in the window is a woman who is leaning against the trunk of a tree. No buildings or roads are in view. Countryside is suggested. The view given to the viewer, or onlooker, might be from a path or trail through a sparsely wooded area. The top of the painting has green foliage, the tree's leaves. Light siphoning through the leaves tells of an assumed sun in a clear sky. The woman and the ground before the woman are dappled, tufts of grass on the ground. The dappling suggests movement, as if there were a breeze.

The woman is in a one-piece dress with a vague pattern on the fabric, a summer garment, bottom hem of which she is beginning to lift. She is posing, but this understanding the viewer comes to slowly, thus a discovery, which means she is posing for someone who has the viewer's perspective, and it would be easy to assume it is the painter. But then . . . maybe the painting is about the woman posing for someone other than the painter, and the painter has depicted this.

She is about mid-thirties and her auburn hair falls mostly in back of her head, but there are traces that lie in front over a shoulder. Her expression is noncommittal, no smile, no frown, but there is questioning on her face, as if she were asking what next. The fulcrum of the picture is suggestion.

A relatively well-dressed couple has wandered up to admire the painting alongside Diane and Wayne, scent of cologne and perfume wafting lightly. They are late middle-aged and they are heavy, but not as heavy as the couple in the café at the foot of Montmartre, the Moulin Rouge couple. Yet it's not exactly weight that distinguishes them from the Moulin Rouge couple. It is bearing, for they have a lighter, more sophisticated touch.

After standing for some moments, which indicates that they are really looking at the painting, the man, in accented English, German or Eastern European, says, "It is a lovely piece, is it not?"

But who is he talking to? The woman next to him or Diane and/or Wayne?

"Yes," Diane says, "it is a lovely picture."

Everyone looks at Diane, including Wayne, but the couple look at Diane in a conversational way, while Wayne looks at Diane in wonderment, for she has attached an accent onto her English, an accent belonging to someone who is French.

"We are thinking of purchasing it," the man says. "But it is dear."

"A minor consideration," Diane rejoins, "considering . . ." She gestures to indicate the painting.

"We need to arrive at a decision," the man continues, "because this painting will not be here forever."

Diane turns to look at the man directly, and she says, "What do you mean?"

"It will be bought by someone such as yourselves who want to possess the splendor of art."

"The splendor of art," Diane enunciates.

"Yes," the woman says, her first words, or word.

Diane looks at the woman, but then turns to face the painting, which directs everyone's attention in that direction—the painting.

"This woman too," Diane says, French accent continuing, "is contemplating splendor."

The four of them stand with the painting before them.

"My lover and I will soon return to our room," Diane relates, "and in walking to our room we will think of this woman. We will take her with us."

"So," says the man, "you do not intend to purchase this picture?"

"We already possess it," Diane says. "There is no need to buy it. All that remains is to enact its splendor."

The man smiles, cheeks fleshy and clean-shaven and reddish. The woman next to him has a puzzled look on her face, and it is only that expression that distinguishes her face from the man's.

"We must be off," Diane says and takes Wayne by the arm.

SEVENTEEN

The café across from their hotel is still open. But all the other shops along the street have darkened. Diane looks at the café and leans forward as if to peer into it, yet this is hardly practical because they are across the street and are about to go through the doorway of their hotel. A sense of foreboding is on Diane's face.

"Do you see him?" Diane asks, voice half-whisper and half-hiss, a combination of fear and repulsion. "The evil man."

Wayne says, "No. Do you?"

"Let us go in there and have a glass of beer and if he's in there I'll go to our room and get the seriated knife and return and stick it in his fat neck."

Wayne looks at her in astonishment.

They cross the street and enter the café. Wayne's legs feel like sticks. They go straight to the bar and Diane orders. Wayne looks around the room, which is well lit but not glaringly lit. Only one other customer is standing at the bar, a woman who is well into middle age, face with a lot of makeup, hair dark and dry and sticking out here and there. A stemmed glass with clear liquid, probably white wine, is on the bar in front of the woman along with a pamphlet she is looking at. Her eyes are sunken in a wealth of mascara.

A group of eight people, men and women, occupy three tables that have been shoved together, half the group on a padded bench along a wall, the others on chairs opposite those on the bench. Wine bottles and glasses are part of the configuration as is conversation.

Two glasses of beer arrive. The barman retreats. Wayne looks at the beer, and it looks so good because his mouth is so dry. Diane picks up her glass and Wayne picks up his. There is no toast. They simply drink, Wayne vigorously, for the beer tastes as good as it looks.

"She is waiting for him, waiting for the evil man," Diane says and gestures with a nod toward the woman with the heavy makeup who's at the bar on the other side of Wayne. Wayne doesn't need to turn to look because he has already looked at the woman and he imagines she is still the same—glass of white wine and a pamphlet. Menace is in Diane's voice, a whispered voice.

"Maybe we should leave," Wayne suggests.

"Let us finish our beer. Maybe the evil man will show up, which will allow me to deal with him."

Wayne sips his beer, but it doesn't taste the same as it did a moment ago.

"I'll pay and we can get out of here," Wayne says.

"Okay, but wait a sec."

Diane walks past Wayne and comes up to the woman and says something in French. Wayne has turned to watch. The woman's face crinkles up and she says something back to Diane. Diane makes a quick, abrupt motion with her hand while saying something to the woman. The woman says something back to Diane in a high thin voice that gets the attention of the barman who walks over to place two thick hands on the bar's surface, pamphlet and wineglass nearby.

The barman is looking at Diane and he is saying something that Diane doesn't seem to like because Diane is raising her voice and waving a hand in response, which initiates a further response from the barman and a response from the woman as well.

Wayne hurries over while digging money out of his pocket. He holds the money out for the barman to take, which gives pause to the argument. The barman takes a bill from Wayne's hand. While returning the rest of the money to his pocket Wayne takes Diane by the elbow with his free hand to urge her away from the confrontation and toward the doors of the café. The group of eight people at the three tables watch Wayne guide Diane out of the café.

Out on the street Wayne says, "What the hell were you trying to do in there?"

Diane doesn't reply.

She only walks alongside Wayne as if each step were mechanical. They come to the door of their hotel and climb the stairs, sounds of their shoes echoing. In the mini-lobby no one is behind the counter. They continue up another stairway to the next floor and enter their room.

"Ahhhh," intones Diane after the door is closed and a light turned on. Her shoulders are suddenly relaxed, her face aglow, her body bouncy. All the rancor is gone as she takes off her red beret and flings it like a Frisbee onto the bed's patchwork bedspread.

"I must shower," Diane reports and heads for the bathroom.

"Wait a minute," Wayne says. "I have to pee."

"Okay, go ahead and pee. Have a long, drawn-out piss. Empty your bladder, but leave your ball-sacks full." She smiles.

Wayne does a double take, for Diane's transformation, even with the day's events, is surreal. How could the same woman, the same person, look and sound so different as compared to just minutes before? A mystery. Wayne enters the bathroom with that mystery in his head.

After coming out of the bathroom, Wayne gets a bottle of Kronenbourg from the refrigerator. Diane enters the bathroom. Wayne soon hears the soft, steady sound of a shower. At the window, Wayne looks out and sips his beer. Something catches his eye. It's the man with the yellow shirt and thick neck. He's going into the café. A twitch travels up Wayne's spine.

Wayne looks toward the bathroom door and sees that it's closed. He then looks at the table where the remains of cheese and bread and olives sit like a still life, serrated knife part of the picture. He looks out the window again. The evil man is no longer visible. Obviously he is in the café. Wayne takes a sip of beer, tension along his backbone settling, but there is something stirring in his mind, a notable image, and it's not the evil man or the café, and it isn't Diane, either.

Wayne takes another sip of beer and turns slowly, eyes going around the room until they alight on the table with the leftover food. He steps over for a closer look. A postcard is on the table, seemingly on top of the Monet card. Wayne presumes that the Courbet postcard, *The Origin of the World*, is gone and is in little pieces in the café with the Toulouse-Lautrec poster where Diane embarrassed the couple who had been to the Moulin Rouge.

The postcard Wayne now looks at is *La Source* (The Source), which is often entitled *The Spring* in English, as in water that flows from the earth as opposed to the season. Its creator is Ingres, a work he completed in 1856 after having begun it thirty-six years earlier. Ingres, along with a few assistants, finished it when Ingres was seventy-six years old, and by then Ingres was a celebrated artist.

Wayne understands that it isn't just the postcard on the table that has lodged itself in his mind. It is the painting itself as it hangs in the Orsay, an image that has been resurrected because of the postcard. And so now they go back and forth—the postcard and the painting in the museum. *La Source* is a distinctly vertical rendition of a young woman, its verticality twice its width. It is over five feet tall. The young woman is completely naked and she is holding a large ceramic jug over her left shoulder and a flow of water is coming out of the jug and is running over her left hand, which is supporting the jug at its wide mouth. Water continues to flow over and past her hand all the way to the bottom of the painting where it flattens out to shine like a shallow puddle. The woman's facial expression is neutral, as if she were far away, yet she is posing for the viewer, the painter. Her right arm is lifted and goes over her head so that her hand can steady the jug on her shoulder, armpit yawning and hairless. The woman's pubic area is the same, smooth and hairless. Wayne stands like he did at the museum, looking at the postcard . . . looking at the painting.

Wayne returns to the window and looks out. A worker from the café is bringing in the tables and chairs that are outside. The place is closing up. Wayne sips his beer and waits for the man with the thick neck to come out of the café. Maybe the middle-aged woman who Diane got into an argument with will be with the man. Of course they might have already left. Wayne could have missed them when he was at the table looking at the Ingres postcard. Lights are going out in the café. Wayne hears a sound and turns. Diane is coming out the bathroom completely naked and completely new.

Closing the bathroom door, she stands for Wayne to look at. She raises her right hand and swings it up to loop over the top of her head and to dangling above her left shoulder just like in the postcard except there's no jug of water. And like in the postcard, and the painting at the Orsay, her yawning armpit is hairless.

Wayne can't remember if there was hair there before, but he can certainly remember that her pubic mound had hair, whereas now there isn't any. She must have shaved herself in the bathroom, but it's more than just that. It's the way she's standing and the way she's looking at something in some middle distance, and yet she's posing for Wayne. Or maybe she's posing for the room or herself or the image that's on the postcard . . . the image that's at the Orsay. Her hair is a different color than the woman's hair that's in the painting and of course Diane isn't so young, but . . . there's that image, that stance, that look in Diane's eyes, a non-focused look, a waiting look. She is attempting a young image and her efforts are not unsuccessful.

Wayne raises his bottle of beer and sips.

Diane now seems to be watching. Wayne lowers the bottle and looks at Diane. Diane averts her eyes, and with this she brings her arm back from over her head and takes a couple of steps toward Wayne, shyness abounding. She brings a hand to the bottle of beer, which Wayne lets her have. She sips from the bottle and then lowers it.

"How refreshing," she says.

That's the image—refreshing. Wayne wants to touch her. This is foreplay. But this brand of foreplay is not the means to something else. It is of itself. It is its own end. Its pleasure is not defined by what's next. Its enjoyment is in each moment, which is confined to not knowing what's next.

Diane holds the bottle out for Wayne to take, so he takes it. She reaches past him and closes the curtains without looking out the window. She walks to the refrigerator and gets out a bottle of beer and uncaps it. She sips, and after she swallows she says to Wayne, "Take off your clothes and be the Hunchback."

So he does. Naked and with his arms hanging down and his back bent and his head turned sideways he looks at Diane with a slightly upward angle. Diane remains across the room, next to the small refrigerator. Wayne's face is twisted, mouth pulled down on one side. He takes a couple of faltering steps, swaying, while not moving in any direction. His bottle of beer sits on the bedside table.

Diane watches him. She seems pleased and looks at the full-length mirror that's on the wall next to the bedside table. Wayne turns awkwardly and looks at the mirror too. He sways back and forth in front of the mirror. Diane takes a couple of steps to her left, which puts her in line with the mirror, Wayne in foreground, Diane in background. The table with the leftover food is to the left of their images, the bed to the right. Diane walks over and carefully squeezes past Wayne so as not to touch him. In front of the mirror Diane drinks from the bottle of beer in her hand and then holds it out for Wayne. Wayne takes the bottle from her and drinks crookedly.

Diane reaches and picks up a piece of bread, which is dried out like the other pieces of bread on the table. She pushes the bread against Wayne's mouth and says, "Eat."

Wayne tries to eat the bread from her hand. He's an animal that she's feeding. She giggles. The bread is gone, crumbs on the floor, Wayne chewing.

"Sit," she says and pats the edge of the bed.

He sits down and leans crookedly. Diane gets a condom from the bedside table and tears its wrapper off.

EIGHTEEN

They lie on the bedspread side by side. Her head rests on his outstretched arm and they gaze upward in exhaustion. It's a relaxed mode, whereas moments before they were panting, air going in and out of their lungs, chests heaving. Wayne reaches for the bottle of beer that's on the bedside table. He reached for it twice during their frantic activity too, but in that reaching and drinking there was no grace. Now, though, there is decency. Diane was of the same ilk, no elegance. But now there's elegance as she rises up to take the bottle from him and sip.

"We need cold beer," she tells him. "A cold bottle of beer."

Wayne heads for the refrigerator, barefoot and naked. A soft beige washes the room, bedside lamp accounting for this. Wayne returns with the opened bottle of beer and offers Diane the first sip. She takes the bottle from him. Wayne stands next to the bed, watching her. Diane's eyes gather moisture, a reaction from the fizziness of the beer in her mouth. Wayne can taste the beer as he sees it in her expression and in her eyes. Wayne glances at the floor and sees the condom as it lies on the carpet all shriveled and moist. He gets back on the bed and sits cross-legged and accepts the bottle of beer from Diane.

Diane assumes the same position. Cross-legged and nude, they face one another. The bottle of beer goes back and forth. The street outside is quiet. It's early a.m.

"I must pee," Diane reckons and gets off the bed and goes into the bathroom, but she doesn't close the door, and neither does she turn on the light.

Wayne listens to urine hitting the water in the toilet bowl. A long stream. He realizes he, too, has to piss. He waits for Diane to emerge and when she does Wayne gets off the bed and goes into the bathroom and leaves the door open and doesn't turn on the light. There is light enough from the beige light coming from the lamp next to the bed. The flushing from Diane's flushing the toilet is settling into a peaceful silence, but this is interrupted by Wayne's splashing, which is probably louder than Diane's because he is standing. Is she listening?

He finishes and flushes the toilet and comes out of the bathroom. Diane is on the bed like before, cross-legged, no clothes. Wayne thinks to get another bottle of beer, so he goes to the refrigerator. On the bedside table there are three empty or nearly empty bottles. When Wayne comes up to the bed he sees there is a postcard on the bedspread in front of Diane. He gives her the bottle of beer and then he looks down at the postcard to see what the picture is, but it's hard to see exactly what's on the postcard because the colors are blue and green and beige, and the light from the lamp is a weak beige.

Wayne sits down on the bed and assumes a cross-legged position, postcard between the two of them on the bedspread. Because the card is upside-down in Wayne's view he has to put it together consciously in his mind to see what kind of images are on the card. When the picture comes together he understands that he's looking at *Thatched Cottages at Cordeville* by Vincent van Gogh, 1890, a painting he looked at in the Orsay.

"He did this," Diane begins, "in Auvers-sur-Oise, a town to the north of Pairs. This painting was completed a couple of weeks before his death."

Diane hands the bottle of beer to Wayne. He takes it and sips.

"Notice the impasto, the thick paint," Diane says and turns the card to face Wayne.

"The twisted house," Diane says. "The swirling sky, the reeling cypress trees. It's a storm. But is it a storm upon the land or a storm in Vincent's mind?"

Wayne looks up from the card.

"A landscape," Diane relates. "Yet so alive, so absolutely alive. Would this have been possible without the distortion? Would it have been so vibrant?"

Wayne looks down at the card.

"Where does the landscape end and Vincent begin?" Diane asks.

Diane reaches over and takes the bottle of beer from him. A long, slow pull from the bottle follows. After lowering the bottle, her free hand drops to her vagina. She inserts a finger. The beer bottle remains in her other hand. Wayne sees imagery in motion.

"Thatched Cottages at Cordeville," Diane says. "How quaint."

The beer bottle comes up and she drinks, her eyes with a certain luster, Wayne a witness. She hands him the bottle and he drinks. Her finger continues inside her although now it's more than a single finger. Her eyes dart. Her un-busy hand goes out to wrap around the back of Wayne's neck and to pull his face to her face where she kisses him like on the street after leaving the park, tongues slithering.

Wayne looks into her eyes. Her eyes are wide. She lets go of his neck and their faces fall away. She is off the bed and standing, legs unsteady, balance a problem. Wayne turns his torso to watch her as she goes to the window where she throws open the curtains and opens the window. She looks left and right, head jerking.

"Hurry," she hisses. "Take me now, take me here, at the edge of the belfry."

And why wouldn't she be sleeping from exhaustion that comes from prolonged frenzy? He stands, looking at her, a supine body curled sideways beneath the bedspread. At the nostrils of her nose, which are pressed lightly on a pillowcase, he detects a tranquil breath. He envies her repose. He turns back to the window and looks out to where lights twinkle one by one on what he supposes is the other side of the river.

He tried to sleep, but couldn't. So he slipped out from under the sheet and bedspread and went to the refrigerator and got the last bottle of beer. Beer in hand, he went to the window and opened the curtains, but left the window closed. He stood naked and sipped beer. He turned to look at her, and now he turns back, window and its view like rumination. In the sky a whisper of gray has begun. Call it a new day. But he wonders where the last day ended. Perhaps it ended when sleep took Diane, because until she fell asleep her intensity was all he had. He couldn't put her aside even for a few moments.

It's only now that he can think on his own, and he thinks about the approaching day. Should he make a plan? He starts to chuckle but stifles it because he doesn't want to make any kind of noise that might wake Diane. A plan for today? What could he possibly plan, even for a day, much less beyond a day? Future seems preposterous.

He turns and looks at her again. She's so beautiful, sleeping. He hopes she doesn't have a nightmare. Certainly nightmares are part of her repertoire. He hopes she continues to sleep. He hopes nothing disturbs her. He hopes he can crawl into bed very soon and fall asleep next to her.

Turning again, he looks out the window and looks downward. The café across the street is dark. It's too early for business. He wonders what time it opens.

NINETEEN

Midday is coming through the window. But it's different than the day before. It's summertime sunlight, full summertime, no holding back. The room is warm and it may soon become hot. Overnight, and what was late spring, a lingering spring, is past.

The sounds entering from the window are harsh. A truck horn, a child crying, the screech of metal on concrete. Someone is dragging something on a sidewalk.

His view is sideways away from the window but he knows the curtains have been drawn to the side and the window is open. Diane is not next to him. He has a clear view of the door that leads to the hallway. Diane is not in view. He hears thick paper, wrapping paper, getting folded and he knows it's in the room and very nearby.

He rolls over and sees Diane at the table where the leftover food was, and "was" is correct because most of what was on the table is gone. He says, "Good morning," and she turns.

"Well, yes," she says and sort of smiles, and says: "Good afternoon."

She has the black vest on, red embroidering lining its hems. The beret is not on her head. It is only the vest that she wears. Her body is very white with the sunlight in back of it.

"Do you have to do wee-wee and brush your teeth?" she asks.

It takes a moment and then he chuckles. It always takes a moment to tune into Diane. He understands it's a new day.

"Yes."

He swings out of bed and walks to the bathroom, naked, as if that were the only way to be in this weather. He enjoys a lengthy piss. He is sore, the soreness of sex, and he wonders if Diane is sore like this too. Brushing his teeth, he feels toothpaste foaming in his mouth. There is something like a hangover at the rear of his head but it's not severe. He glances to the side and realizes he left the bathroom door open. Or did he? Diane enters his peripheral view. She's in the doorway, but Wayne's view is flawed because he's bent over the sink with the toothbrush working in his mouth. Diane seems to be watching him.

She steps into the bathroom. Wayne is leaning over to bringing water to his mouth with the hand that doesn't have the toothbrush. Water slushes in his mouth. Whitish water then flows out of his mouth into the basin. Diane is next to him. Wayne straightens while rinsing the toothbrush in tap water. He puts the toothbrush down. Diane hands him a hand towel. Wayne dries his hands and wipes his mouth with the towel. Diane is so close. Wayne sees her face next to his face in the mirror that's above the basin. She looks in the mirror to look at him and they look at each other in the mirror. They watch as Wayne gets aroused. It's an after-a-long-sleep arousal, slow and thick. Diane seems to know more about this than he does.

"A little sore, are we?" she says. Her fingers are delicate.

"This way," she says. "I will sit on the table for you."

She leads him out of the bathroom by the hand to where the table has been cleared, perhaps for this purpose. She sits on the edge of the table. In addition to her buttocks there is a condom on the table. Wayne removes the wrapper from the condom and unfurls it along his erection. Diane spreads her legs and leans back to rest on her elbows. She looks at Wayne as he advances. There is the summer light coming into the room accompanied by the indiscriminate sounds of a city.

Diane and Wayne languish in a slow rhythm. Wayne glances at the window and sees a milky blue sky. Diane asks for a bottle of cold water. Wayne pulls away and goes to the small refrigerator and gets a plastic bottle of water. He returns to Diane and hands her the bottle. She drinks while looking at him. She hands the bottle back to him and he drinks. A new Diane, a new day, a new season.

With the bottle set on the table, condensation begins on the bottle's sides. Wayne rubs a hand over the bottle and then rubs that hand on Diane's chest. A gasp springs from her throat, but then settles into enjoyment at the surprise that the cold wet hand has brought to her sensitive mounds. She laughs, head thrown back, and when that finishes there is a moment of something else that culminates in her torso rising to where she hooks her hands over Wayne's shoulders and pulls and pushes, and Wayne understands, for it is the intimacy of selfish intent.

"Brioche!" she tells him while standing with a hand raised, gesture of an instant idea, room languid. "We need brioche from the bakery."

"Okay."

"And a couple of large cups of coffee from that Starbucks-like place on the corner."

"Right."

"A wedge of cheese. Red cheddar."

"I'll try."

"Raspberry jam. A little jar."

"Got it."

He gets dressed and is out the door and on his way downstairs. The front-desk clerk gives him a "Hello" and he returns the greeting.

Out on the street it is what he expected, heat coupled with the tightness of humidity as if the Seine were secreting. It seems too early in the year for this, but then again May has turned into June, but still . . . it seems premature. As he weaves his way through people and cars he concludes that he doesn't mind it. He could stay in Paris amid its stifling summer because Diane has defined its attractions.

Entering a bakery with its wonderful aroma, he feels empty, as if he's been drained, yet at the same time there's this lightness and bounciness to his step, and whatever hangover he had is now gone.

After waiting his turn, he gestures and uses his fingers as counters. The stout woman waiting on him understands. She gives a toothy smile and announces the price with fingers of her own, brioche going into a paper sack. It is when he is reaching into his pocket for the money that he discovers a postcard. So along with some euro bills he brings the card out. He gives the woman money, which she takes with a swipe, *"Merci"* concurrent. He has the paper bag in one hand and the card in the other as he jostles his way out of the shop.

On the narrow sidewalk in front of the shop he looks at the card and he sees that it's *Alone*, by Toulouse Lautrec, 1896, oil on cardboard, in what is considered a "study," but how complete the picture is while maintaining a feel of spontaneity—prostitute lying on her back on a bed with her black-stockinged legs hanging over the edge of the bed from the knees down. Is she relaxing or exhausted? Perhaps both. Is this from memory or is Lautrec in the room? If he's in the room, he's so acquainted with her that she pays him no mind, for there's the title of the piece—*Alone*.

Wayne is startled because the title snaps at him.

He immediately starts for the hotel, but then he slows when he thinks about the shopping list. He stops and looks down the block. People seem to be on their lunchbreak, yet it seems too late for that. Lunch ought to be over by now. He looks upward and tries to see the window of his and Diane's room, but he's too far away to distinguish that. Looking down at the postcard, he sees what he saw before: Lautrec's study/painting of a slim woman on her back and draped over a messy bed. He turns the card over. The reverse side is blank except for some notation about the painting, oil on cardboard and etcetera. He thinks about cardboard with oil paint on it, and again, as in the Orsay, Wayne's eyes tell him that it's a finished painting. But what the hell is he thinking about? This piece displays: "alone."

Again he starts for the hotel, and again he stops. If she's leaving him, she's already gone because she would have known that when he paid for the first purchase he would find the card. Of course she put the card in his pants' pocket. He has never seen this card before. He's certain of that. The actual painting, yes, at the Orsay. He stands with the revelation that he does not want to lose Diane.

He gulps. The cheese store is across the street. He goes over there to buy a wedge of cheese because it doesn't make any difference. At least this is what his mind is telling him. Diane is either already gone or she's not going to be gone. He picks up a piece of orange cheese wrapped in cellophane and turns to look at shelves lined with jars. He selects a small jar that seems to be raspberry jam. A slim man in a white lab coat rings the items up and accepts Wayne's money. Wayne has tucked the postcard in a side pocket of his cargo pants.

Out on the sidewalk he walks in the opposite direction from where his hotel is. The Starbucks-like place is at the end of the block. The sidewalk is crowded and people have stepped into the street to walk. People are mindful of passing cars. Wayne, too, steps into the street. He can make better time that way. Where did all these people come from? Were they here yesterday? He doesn't think so, or maybe he didn't notice.

At the coffee shop he discovers he's going to have to wait in line. He looks at the card again. He keeps looking at it while waiting in line. When he gets to the counter he has to make a choice about what kind of coffee to order. Diane only designated, "large."

He chooses café au lait because that's what people drink in France, or so he thinks. Also, he can pronounce it. The woman waiting on him is astonishingly young and astonishingly beautiful. She knows how to say: "small, medium, or large." She is astonishingly kind.

Wayne motions to indicate he wants them to go. She understands perfectly. She says, "To go." Wayne can't believe it. She's bilingual. He pays. She offers instructions by way of pointing to where Wayne can pick up his order. Wayne says, "*Merci.*" She smiles and it's astonishing.

Does he have everything? Yes, he has everything—brioche, cheese, jam, coffee. He trots down the street in what is either excitement or anxiety. He can't wait to get back to his room. Will it be joy or will it be devastation?

TWENTY

When he opens the door he understands that Diane is in the room. He knows it before he sees her. He knows it by the feel of the room. Her presence is in the room. Her intensity is in the room.

She is standing in front of the full-length mirror. She turns from looking at the mirror. She is dressed, one of the dresses she bought the day before—a summer dress.

"Let us eat," she says. "Then we will depart for Wien."

"Wien?" questions Wayne.

"Vienna."

"Vienna? In Austria?"

"That is correct."

"Why?"

"To see Klimt. The *Beethoven Frieze*."

He smiles hesitatingly and says, "Okay."

"Come and sit down and we will eat." Diane motions toward the table.

They sit down and the provisions are laid out, nothing said about the choice of coffee or cheese or jam. That's all that's on the table, food and drink. But of course the serrated knife is on the table too, a constant for slicing bread or cheese, or spreading jam or butter. They begin eating and drinking.

Wayne gets the postcard out of his pocket and places it on the table, picture-side up. Diane looks at it and picks it up with her fingers. She turns the card over and looks at the reverse side.

"Lautrec," she says and sets the card down. She puts a piece of brioche in her mouth.

Wayne is looking at her, but all she shows him is her closed mouth with her jaw muscles working as she chews. The fresh brioche has scented the room. Afternoon heat is asserting itself. Wayne stands up and starts for the window because it seems to be shut. The curtains are drawn closed.

"Don't go to the window!"

Wayne stops and turns. "Why?"

"That evil monster, the one causing all the problems, car crashes and so forth, is down there in that café. We don't want him to know we're here."

Wayne returns to the table and sits down. Diane's eyes go to the knife. Wayne looks at the knife. Then he looks at the card.

"Do you know anything about this card?" Wayne asks.

"Yes. It's a marvelous painting by Lautrec. It's in the Orsay. But of course you know that. We took a long time looking at it yesterday."

"I found it in my pocket. The postcard."

"Oh?"

Diane sips her coffee. After she swallows she looks down at the knife.

"We'll take the knife with us when we leave," Diane says. "I'll put it in my pocket. There's a nice deep pocket on one side of my dress."

"What do we need the knife for?"

"In case he comes out of the café when we're leaving. When we're coming out of the doorway onto the sidewalk he might be coming out of the café and he might see us."

Diane picks up her cup of coffee.

"How about if I carry the knife?" Wayne says.

"No, darling, it has to be me."

The use of "darling" is new. Wayne breaks off a piece of cheese and puts it in his mouth and chews. He thinks about "darling."

"As soon as we finish our lunch we'll pack. We'll put everything in the suitcase we bought yesterday." She gestures, but Wayne doesn't turn around to look.

"Your things and my things," Diane says. "That way we'll only have the one small case to carry. You can carry it."

"We won't be able to fit your things and my things in there. And besides, what's wrong with my bag? It has wheels."

"Well," Diane says, "what we can't fit in the *nice* suitcase we'll put in your *modern* suitcase, and we'll leave your modern suitcase in the outdoor seating area across the street."

"What do you mean?"

"The nice suitcase we will take with us to Wien, and your not-nice suitcase we'll leave across the street. So the things we really want to take with us will go in the nice suitcase, and everything else will go in the not-nice suitcase."

Diane puts a piece of cheese in her mouth. Wayne watches her chew and wonders about everything she has told him.

"Imagine," Diane says, "Klimt and the *Beethoven Frieze*. Also, Egon Schiele is in Wien. We'll take one of those super-fast trains and we'll arrive in Wien today. We'll check into a hotel and have dinner. A substantial dinner—schnitzel. We'll be tired and full, and we'll sleep like babies. Tomorrow we'll have a piece of delicious chocolate cake and a cup of rich coffee in a café. Then, completely fortified, we'll embark, destination: *Beethoven Frieze* in the Secession building. After that . . ."

"After that, what?"

She seems embarrassed, she seems bashful, she seems. . .

"After that there's no telling."

Wayne has stopped eating. He's listening and looking right at her.

"What we had here in Paris was the beginning, Wayne. There's more."

"Well . . . wait a minute."

"Wait for what?"

"I want to be absolutely clear about what's going to happen."

Diane's emblematic half-smile emerges.

"Well," she begins, "we really never know exactly what's going to happen, do we?"

Wayne moistens his lips with his tongue even though his lips don't need moistening.

"Okay, so the things we want to take, mine and yours, are going into the nice suitcase," Wayne says. "And the things we don't want are going into my not-nice suitcase."

"That's right, and just to add a little something else, I'm going to put those spent condoms that are in the trash in the not-nice suitcase to go along with our not-nice clothes."

Wayne is looking at her.

"After all, we're going to leave this little package, your suitcase, across the street in that outdoor seating area."

"I think we better leave it in the room here," Wayne says. "You leave it in front of the café and they might think it's a bomb or something."

What's left from Diane's half-smile is rejuvenating, but it keeps going and becomes a full smile.

"They'll pin it on that evil man in there," Diane says. "He's probably with that bitch. I should have slapped her face last night."

"What?"

"We'll flag a cab at the end of the block where there's traffic. After we're in the cab we might hear sirens, and they'll have him, and they'll have that bitch of a girlfriend of his, right there in the café."

"But there won't be anything . . . There won't be anything in the bag that can explode. It's just a suitcase with some dirty clothes."

"You can never tell. That evil man, like that horrible car wreck yesterday . . . You can never tell."

"But you don't want a bomb over there in the café, do you?"

"We can't control that. We're simply dropping off a suitcase with some spent condoms and old clothes. What happens after that is out of our hands, suitcase or no suitcase. Hopefully, that man will be apprehended."

Wayne sits. The room is hot.

"You didn't put a bomb in my suitcase, did you?"

Diane looks at him.

"What are you talking about, Wayne? Have you lost your mind?"

Wayne reaches for what's left of his coffee. His mouth and throat need moisture.

"Come on, let's start packing. Once we're out of Paris . . . Well, as they say: Out of sight, out of mind—that man and that bitch."

She stands up and strides across the room and goes into the bathroom.

"I just need to get my toothbrush," Diane relays.

Wayne gets to his feet and turns to see Diane coming out of the bathroom, toothbrush in hand. Diane opens the old suitcase and puts the toothbrush in a side pocket of the interior lining. She then steps over to the wastebasket and pulls out the plastic bag that contains trash, used condoms part of it. She puts the trash bag in Wayne's suitcase, and with this Wayne notices that Diane's minimal wardrobe is already in his suitcase, the modern suitcase. Diane's beret and vest and shoulder bag are lying on the bedspread of the bed. Evidently the only thing Diane needs to pack in the old, vintage suitcase is a toothbrush.

Diane walks over to the table that Wayne is standing next to. She picks up the serrated knife and puts it in the pocket of her dress.

"We'll leave the food and things where they are.

Leave a tip for housekeeping, Wayne. Five euros. They've done a marvelous job, not bothering us."

Wayne looks down at the table.

"What about the postcards?"

"They'll be postcards in Wien. Wonderful postcards. Postcards like you've never seen."

ACKNOWLEDGMENTS

I am indebted to Christoph and Leza at CLASH Books for seeing this project through. Thanks ever so much.

ABOUT THE AUTHOR

Michael Onofrey grew up in Los Angeles. Currently he lives in Japan. Over ninety of his short stories have appeared in journals and magazines. Seven stories have been anthologized. A novel, "Bewilderment," was published by Tailwinds Press in 2017.

THE HAUNTING OF THE PARANORMAL ROMANCE AWARDS

Christoph Paul & Mandy De Sandra

GODLESS HEATHENS: CONVERSATIONS WITH ATHEISTS

Edited by Andrew J. Rausch

DARK MOONS RISING IN A STARLESS NIGHT

Mame Bougouma Diene

GODDAMN KILLING MACHINES

David Agranoff

NOHO GLOAMING & THE CURIOUS CODA OF ANTHONY SANTOS

Daniel Knauf (Creator of HBO's Carnivàle)

IF YOU DIED TOMORROW I WOULD EAT YOUR CORPSE

Wrath James White

THE ANARCHIST KOSHER COOKBOOK

Maxwell Bauman

HORROR FILM POEMS

Poetry by Christoph Paul & Art by Joel Amat Güell

NIGHTMARES IN ECSTASY

Brendan Vidito

THE VERY INEFFECTIVE HAUNTED HOUSE

Jeff Burk

www.ingramcontent.com/pod-product-compliance
Lightning Source LLC
Chambersburg PA
CBHW032038180726
48284CB00008B/2641